The Puppet Explained

Dear Angela,

This book teaches
how to making your
own stories ☺

Have fun.

Love,
Bernhard

The Puppet Explained

BRYNN CARTER

authorHOUSE®

AuthorHouse™
1663 Liberty Drive
Bloomington, IN 47403
www.authorhouse.com
Phone: 1-800-839-8640

Published by AuthorHouse   03/17/2012

ISBN: 978-1-4685-5617-9 (sc)
ISBN: 978-1-4685-5616-2 (e)

Library of Congress Control Number: 2012903319

CONTENTS

CHAPTER 1

Who Are They?

MISS MUFFET

They probably like my blue hair best. At least that is what they usually notice first. Someone will say, "Oh, she has BLUE hair!" and they will all giggle. Then they see the sparkle in my eyes, and think I am alive, and can tell I have something to say. That is when I clear my throat just a little bit, and very politely introduce myself by name. I usually like to call their attention to my clothing by quietly asking, "Do you like my pink, dotted-Swiss skirt?" I gracefully twist just a bit, so its fullness can swish around me two or so times. And of course, they all do like my skirt; even the boys. Then I sit down carefully, and use my hands to smooth my skirt, making sure it shows nicely, without a tuck or rumple. And of course, I will feel my hair to be certain it is in place and that I am appearing at my best for them. Then I will look to see how many are there. I will look straight out, moving my head slowly from left to right, and then back again, so I do not miss anyone. Then I will tip my head up just a bit so I can see those in the back, or lean out a smidgen and look down, so I can also see those who are seated up close. I almost always can not help but notice a few individuals, and find myself staring directly at one person about a moment too long. Everyone can tell that I am staring, and then they all look at that person, too, until it is silly. Then they look back at me, and by then I am embarrassed, and cover my face with my hands, but I still seem to do it every time, to at least one of them.

SPIDER

That's when I begin to appear from out of nowhere, but I'm nothing special. My eyes do catch the light, but I'm not sparkly, or shiny. In fact, my body is a ball, coated with flat, black paint. Still, wouldn't you know it, even when I'm t o t a l l y quiet, and just show myself real cautiously, so as not to distract, they always see me right away. Maybe it's because they've been focused on her pink, dotted Swiss, and I've got long, hairy legs. I don't know. It's just they always notice me, but she never does. You know, they'll point and start getting out of their chairs to make her pay attention to me. Darn if it doesn't just take a long, long time. So, I wait; it's good manners. Did I mention that I wear a handsome blue hat? Well, I do. And I know it's polite to remove my hat in the presence of a lady. That's why I've got this nifty mechanism all rigged up with clear fishing line, so when she finally does turn around, I can tip my hat courteously. But I ask you, "What do you think is going to happen next?". . .

Yes, and it happens, *every* time.

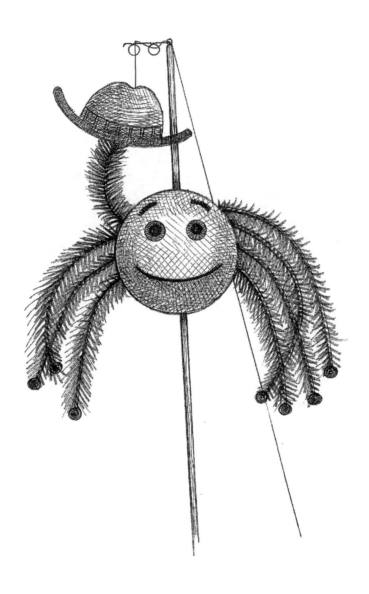

PROFESSOR

Readers, may I have your attention please. The preceding was provided as introduction to the topics that we will consider throughout the following pages. That being said, allow me to briefly introduce myself. My credentials are impressive and I will most definitely speak with authority on the subjects with which you will soon become engaged. I have been described as an eloquent speaker. Furthermore, it's been said that use of my hands in gestures or emphasis effectively enhances communication. I hope you will not find the fact that I wear spectacles to be distracting, even though they do sometimes slip down to the tip of my nose, which may cause me to look stern or disapproving on occasions, but fortunately, as previously indicated, I am adept with my hands, due to rather clever manipulations by rods, and can therefore readjust my glasses before moving on with the lecture. Humbly, I do admit to appearing rather like Professor Einstein, but what hair remains on my head is much darker than was his. Yes, I am somewhat bald, owing to an idiosyncratic manner for scratching my head. I expect, however, that you will tolerate head scratching, as it is something done by those of us who wonder, ponder and contemplate. Indeed, as we proceed with conversations about story elements, you will occasionally be encouraged to perform head scratching in a repeat-after-me fashion.

And now, I suggest that we begin our dialogue with consideration of what may be the most profoundly important story element, that being *character*. And to introduce the topic of character, it is my recommendation that we begin with a brief theatrical performance. Actually, it will be a play similar to one performed in the 1970s for a university theater arts class. The instructor for that course, an accomplished puppeteer named Betsy Brown, encouraged her students to share the play with others, and it is my pleasure to do so. Therefore, I call your attention to an area just ahead which will function as our stage.

A sign appears. Silver, glitter letters announce the title of a play,

How to Make a Puppet.

The sign is removed and a bare hand appears. Bending from the wrist, it bows elegantly to the audience several times, making sure to bow center, right, center, left, and center. Then, in a wait-a-minute gesture with pointer finger extended, the hand is elevated slightly and pauses in that position, silently communicating, "You wait and I'll be back." The hand turns, and calmly walks off stage.

The hand returns, carrying a second hand, which is flopped onto the stage floor, lifeless.

The first hand again gestures, "Wait a minute" and then leaves, returning with a simple fabric costume, and helps the lifeless hand to stand and begin to dress. Somehow, the initially limp hand becomes a puppet and is very much alive, tall and straight, clapping with excitement, admiring itself, and strutting for the audience to notice, until this puppet realizes that it has no head.

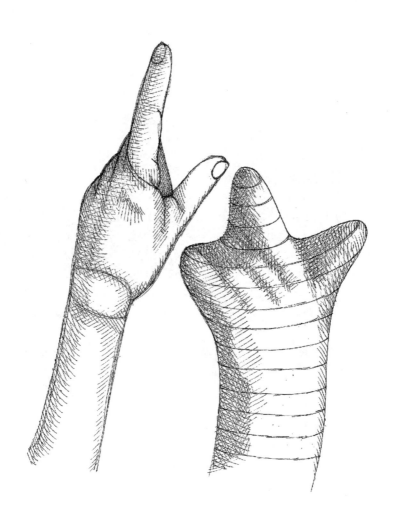

The hand gestures, "Wait a minute" and returns with a four-inch Styrofoam ball. (A finger-size hole has already been cut into the ball.) The hand holds this ball steady, as the puppet folds in its arms, bends at the waist, and readies to ram its neck into the head.
The puppet may miss a time or two, but then manages to acquire a head, and obviously feels proud of it.

"Wait a minute," is again gestured by the hand. It leaves the stage and returns with a small package containing facial features and hair, affixed to tacks that can be pushed into the Styrofoam head. While the puppet's back is to his audience, the hand dramatically and carefully begins to give the puppet features, at first, adding just one eye. The puppet turns around to face the audience; it is a Cyclops. "Oh, no," gestures the puppet, "This will never do!" The puppet turns to face the hand, who affixes a second eye, after which the puppet shows itself to the audience for approval.

Sometimes an eye will dislodge, fall to the stage floor, and then to the audience beyond. When this happens, the hand will gesture to one person in the audience, "You. Please pick up that eye. Put it up here on the stage." Then there is applause for the one who assists.

With eyes in place, the puppet is given a nose, and turns to show the audience and receive approval.

Next comes the mouth, which is a definite curve, but placed up-side-down in a frowny-face way. When the puppet turns to show the audience, again it's, "Oh, no! This will never do!" So the hand adjusts the mouth curve until our puppet is smiling, and can show the audience its happy face.

Eventually comes the hair, which is a silly color and has lots of movement when the puppet tosses its head.

Not yet done, the hand once more gestures, "Wait a minute." It returns with a bowl of face powder and a puff. Then the hand dramatically poofs powder onto the puppet's face, and dust flies all around. In the process, sometimes an eye or other feature will dislodge, and fall down to the audience, and the hand will solicit assistance from someone.

Finally a handsome puppet is facing the audience for admiration and the hand goes off stage to get a mirror. The hand then gives this mirror to the puppet while it is facing the audience. The puppet admires itself, and then turns around so the audience can view a reflection in the mirror, and they will laugh because it is so funny to see a puppet looking in a mirror.

Satisfied, the mirror is laid on the stage floor. The hand and puppet stand side-by-side, hand-to-hand (thumb-to-thumb) facing their audience to take bows, and then clap for each other, blow kisses, etc., before they turn, and again, hand-in-hand, walk off stage.

A sign appears. Silver, glitter letters announce: *The End*

BIG LEFTY

Okay, that's cool. Whoop! Whoop! Whoop! Good puppet play! Right on, Man. I can visualize it. Except there's one thing you failed to make clear, and I'm here to straighten that out. Okay? So, my name is Big Lefty. And my point is that the character who turned into a *puppet* dude was not the ONLY puppet in your play. What about the *hand*? I say he was a puppet, too. He was doing all the work and he was a great actor. So, he didn't have any speaking lines; he was still an awesome actor!

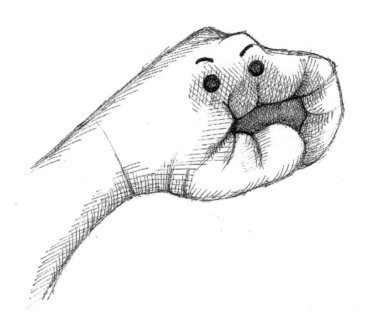

So, like I said, my name is Big Lefty. And yes, a lot of the time, I just look like a hand; you know, at the end of somebody's arm. No big deal. But when I feel like it, I have lots to say. I have a mouth, and I use it; like right now, when I mean to set this straight.

Okay. So that second hand that was in that play, you know the one that just laid there like lifeless at first. Just when did it become a *puppet*, anyway? When it got dressed? When it got some facial features like a mouth or something?

I've got a mouth. I've got it all the time. Sometimes, I even use make up. But other times, I want to be cool, Man; ya know? Lay low, hide out, look like every other hand. But I've still got a mouth and I'm still Big Lefty whenever I feel like it.

MISS MUFFET
Hmm. Hmm. Excuse me, Mr. Lefty. I was just sitting over here, and I did not notice you over there until I heard your voice, which caught my attention. Then I saw your mouth moving, and now I can not help but staring. And I find myself wondering what you might say next.

BIG LEFTY
How about, "Nice hair." Or, "What's with the skirt?" You think they give you personality or something?

MISS MUFFET
Oh. Well, I believe that you can tell something about one's character from appearance. That is why I usually try to look my best. As for your question about "when" the second hand, the one that at first was flopped on the stage and was lifeless, became a puppet, I am thinking that it happened when it started to act. What I mean is, at the beginning, it was just there, and really not worth noticing. The first hand even had to make it stand. But then, the second hand stood on its own, and sort of wriggled its way into the fabric costume, and by that time it was, well, alive.

BIG LEFTY
Okay, yeah; it was alive. But it had like NO personality. So it was moving around inside some fabric. What is so interesting about that?

MISS MUFFET
Well, perhaps the way it moved? Or when it moved? Perhaps it was how the puppet moved in response to the hand? I am not sure, but somehow, I did find myself getting interested in what was happening, and curious about what might happen next. It is kind of like when I toss my blue hair around, and say, "Hmm. Hmm," very sweetly, and fold my hands on my lap. Others always notice, and they start to wonder what I might do next.

PROFESSOR
Permit me to shed some light on this dialogue.

MISS MUFFET
Oh, please do! I love light. It makes the sequins in my eyes sparkle so everyone thinks that I am, well, alive.

PROFESSOR
What I meant was, permit me to provide you with some information so that this conversation, rather than going on and on without clarity, can become a meaningful discourse. I suggest that rather than quibble about when a hand became a puppet, you should first have comprehension about what is denotatively meant by the term "puppet", and therefore I refer you to Webster's New Collegiate Dictionary, albeit, a 1977 copyright. It says,

> 1 a: a small-scale figure (as of a person or animal) usually with a cloth body and hollow head that fits over and is moved by the hand b: MARIONETTE 2: DOLL 3 : one whose acts are controlled by an outside force or influence",

and with that definition, you will be better prepared to continue.

BIG LEFTY

Dude, not trying to disrespect, Man, but that was *bore* ing. I didn't wanta do the stereotype thing, just because you're bald and wear funny glasses, but Dude, you stepped in it. And geeze, whatta lame definition for puppet. Look, Man, I could pick up this here stick, and move it around and make it talk in some, ya know, weird way, and that'd *constitute* a puppet, Man. A piece of junk could constitute a puppet, Dude.

PROFESSOR

"Constitute" a puppet. Interesting.

SPIDER

Excuse me. Miss, I hope I didn't startle you, and won't frighten you away. I'm tipping my blue hat out of respect, Miss, and will hold it above my head until you feel comfortable, or maybe for longer if the fishing line gets stuck, and that's okay with you, Miss. I just want to say that I think appearance is very important to a character. Take me, for example. All I have to do is appear at the corner of the stage, and I'm noticed right away. I can move carefully, without disturbing anything, and speak with a real nice tone of voice and correct grammar, and still they're going to try and warn you about me. It happens time, after time, after time.

MISS MUFFET

Oh. I know. I mean, I remember. I am so sorry.

BIG LEFTY

Hey, Man. That is like outrageously unfair. Talk about stereotyping. Making a judgment about you based on like what, eight hairy legs? And not even taking into account your actions, or what you have to say? Dude, somebody else should tell them what a nice guy you are at heart, deep inside that round, unshiny, black body.

MISS MUFFET

Oh, here is an idea! What if another character, or maybe a narrator would say something about you.

BIG LEFTY
Like describe the dude? Or tell what he's doing or thinking? You mean like some omniscient voice cluing everyone in to what he's really about as an individual?

MISS MUFFET
Well, it is just an idea. But we should think of something, so that he is not stereotyped like some stock character in a fairy tale--a *boy*, a *princess*, a *king*? Obviously this fine Spider is much more than a spherical body covered with flat black paint, and eight hairy legs. He has good manners. He is polite. And he has shown that consistently. Not to mention his blue hat that he tips so nicely, except when strings get caught in the mechanisms, and that is not his fault. What I mean is that I am starting to recognize Spider as an individual, who has been consistent over time, and I am no longer frightened away by his mere appearance.

SPIDER
Thank you, Miss. That means a lot to me, coming from you.

PROFESSOR
It is my opinion that we should attempt some consultations with others representing a variety of puppet forms and characters, and consider their lamentations and advice before proceeding. One can never do too much preparatory work before commencing on an endeavor.

Indeed, I might hypothesize that those who have lived as different puppet forms, have experienced significantly variant roles, responses, and levels of satisfaction in their careers.

MISS MUFFET
Oh, do you mean find out what some other puppets have to say? That would be very wonderful. I will just sit right over here and listen.

PROFESSOR

Listen and learn from other types of puppets. That is, generally, my suggestion. To that end, let us first of all recognize that there are several distinct categories of puppets, and each particular form, may or may not contribute to an efficient perception of the character being presented.

BIG LEFTY

Okay, Man, so like take a look at that dude over there, the one who looks like a cereal box with eyes. Whoa. It looks like he was cut across the back and folded over. And he's got body parts made outta junk, Man; like he's totally recycled.

SNAPPY

Right. I'm a junque puppet. My name is Accurate N. Concise, but everyone calls me "Snappy." I'm a commentator.

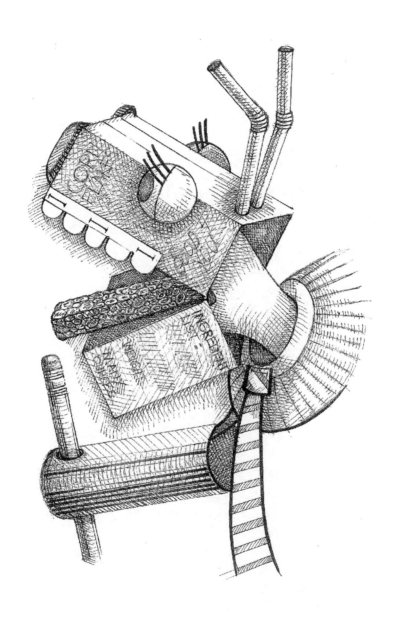

MISS MUFFET
OOOOOh. A "commentator". Really? What exactly is a commentator?

PROFESSOR
Permit me the pleasure of clarifying. Webster's dictionary defines a commentator as "one who reports and discusses news on radio or television." Now, if there is no objection, I would like to address Mr. Concise directly.

Sir, you have already admitted to being a "junque" puppet, and it's readily apparent that you have been constructed from a hodge podge of items that have probably been discarded as no longer useful or attractive; no offense intended.

SNAPPY
None taken. And you can call me Snappy.

PROFESSOR
I appreciate your tolerance, *Snappy*. Now, if I may continue, I was about to state my observation that your construction is certainly out of the ordinary, meaning that you and others like you, could be made from *ANY* thing, and in fact, there are infinite possibilities regarding ways that you might be manipulated. Is that correct?

SNAPPY
Yes.

PROFESSOR
Could you please explain, then, what makes you a puppet, with a distinguishing character.

SNAPPY
Certainly. Accurate N. Concise, here, speaking live from pages of *The Puppet Explained*, confirming that junque puppets are figures that do not necessarily represent a person or animal, yet are controlled by an outside force, in order to communicate to an audience.

To date, there is no authenticated count on the number of junque puppets in existence, but recent trends in recycling and a national outcry for increased attention to the arts in education do indicate that we can expect substantial growth in the junque puppet population. Back to you.

PROFESSOR
Mr. Concise, I mean, *Snappy*, please permit my probing a bit further, as you failed to communicate precisely what makes you a distinguishing character.

SNAPPY
Yes. Certainly. My mouth. Back to you.

BIG LEFTY
Whoa, Dude. Cool mouth, Man. I dig the way it opens and shuts. Cool, Man.

THE PROFESSOR
Mr. Lefty, it appears that you and *Snappy* have something in common, and I am not referring to the obvious fact that both of you have a predominant buccal feature. My observation is more basic and regards something remarkable. It is that you both are capable of movement and communication. And I find this quite intriguing, especially in contrast to that rock situated across the room. It's a stoic form—apparently indifferent to light and social opportunities—indeed unaware and not interesting.

SNAPPY
Well, that's my biz as a commentator—putting a slant on the ordinary to stir up interest. So excuse me folks, while I go to interview Mr. Rock, and work on possibilities for a news story.

BIG LEFTY
Good luck doin' it, Man, 'cause that rock has like no mouth, Man. And unless there's some outside force or influence to get it movin', that stone dude is like staying still over there, outta the lights and alone—not a bubba who's gonna be into conversations, Man. So

I'm like into doing what the Professor said, and checkin' with puppet dudes; you know, ones with like light in their eyes.

MS. UP
YOO HOO! Hello! I'm over here. You probably haven't noticed me, because I'm still inside this container, but if you'll look this direction, you'll see that some of us appear to be regular boxes, and others like cylindrical, oatmeal boxes. You'll notice that we each have a rod extending from the base of our individual box. If you'll push up on my rod, I'll pop up and introduce myself.

SPIDER
I'd be happy to help you. I do want to warn you about my hairy legs though, so you won't be frightened away when you first see them. It might be kind of a shocking surprise if you popped up, and weren't expecting them.

MS. UP
Oh, Golly, thank you for offering to help, and the warning. Actually, I do know a little about the element of surprise, because that's what makes me be so reeeeally much fun. You see, no one ever expects me, and then I pop up and surprise them.

Before I DO pop up, would you like to guess what I look like?

BIG LEFTY
Yeah, Man, I'll bet you look like a small-scale figure of a person.

MISS MUFFET
And perhaps you have wild blue hair and a swirly, pink, dotted-Swiss skirt?

PROFESSOR
Oh, for heaven's sake; that is already quite enough speculation. Someone with knowledge of the subject would understand that a pop-up puppet could resemble any sort of creature, so why continue with this childish guessing game. Indeed, just pop up and let's get on with this discourse about puppet forms and characters.

SPIDER
Alright then. I'm all ready to push up on your rod, if you promise to remember that I warned you about my legs.

MS. UP
Oh, I do!

SPIDER
Then on the count of eight. 1 2 3 4 5 6 7 8!!!

MS. UP
Wow!!! It's really bright out here! Wowie! Zowie! Light everywhere!

MISS MUFFET
Is not light wonderful? Do you love it? I just love how light makes the sequins in my eyes sparkle so everyone thinks I am alive. Oooh! Look, you must be alive, too!!!

PROFESSOR
So, Ms. Up, now that the mechanical means for your upward movement, or the *rod* as it's called, has been pushed, and you have appeared for us, would you be so kind as to elaborate regarding what makes you a distinctive character.

MS. UP
My, how silly; I guess I've never thought about it before.
Sometimes I don't get speaking lines.
Sometimes I pop up and back down quickly. I can be reeeeally fast!
Other times I can appear slowly and cautiously,
OR disappear just a bit . . . at a time . . . looking side . . . to . . . side . . . suspiciously . . . as I descend, and then suddenly POOOF! out of sight.
"a distinctive character" . . . well, I guess I just don't know.

PROFESSOR
Indeed. Thank you, Ms. Up.

MS. UP
You're welcome. I'm happy to just pop up any old time!

BIG LEFTY
Hey, I've got something to say.

MISS MUFFET
Oh, Mr. Lefty. I just love watching you speak. You have such a dominant jaw.

BIG LEFTY
Yeah, right. So what I want to say is about this guy I know who thinks he's a rod puppet. He's really got a swelled head. He's a wooden-spoon dude. So he's got some eyes.

MISS MUFFET
Well, do they sparkle?

BIG LEFTY
Not that I ever saw. He's just a dude with a face and two arms. It's not like he ever moves.

SPIDER
Well, what does he say?

BIG LEFTY
Nothing. That's what I'm telling you. The dude thinks he's a rod puppet, but he's really nothing but a decked-out, wooden spoon.

MISS MUFFET
Well, what do others have to say about him?

BIG LEFTY
Nothing. Zip. My whole point. The dude thinks he's a rod puppet, but he's like nothing. He's like "less than nothing", like that pig said in the story with that lady spider. She wasn't hairy or anything. Sorry, Man, nothing personal. You know the book with the nice lady spider.

SPIDER
Oh, you mean Charlotte. Funny you should mention her. She's my distant cousin.

MISS MUFFET
Mr. Lefty, if the spoon who thinks he is a rod puppet does not do or say anything, and others do not tell what he is like, how can we know anything about his personality?

PROFESSOR
Exactly, Miss Muffet. And your conversation with Mr. Lefty, and I dare say, his line of reasoning, now beg the question: When does an inanimate object, dependent upon control by an outside force or influence, become a puppet that is a distinctive character?

BIG LEFTY
Dude! That's it. Right on, Man. For a grouchy looking, bald guy with funny glasses, maybe you're not so bad, Man. Hey, this heavy, critical-thinking stuff makes me feel like scratching my head, Man. Problem is, I don't have a hand.

SPIDER
Let me help you. I can scratch your head while standing on my seven other legs.

BIG LEFTY
Whoa, Dude; thanks, but I'm really ticklish.

PROFESSOR
Mr. Lefty, may we infer from your stated inclination to "scratch your head", that you are in fact beginning to wonder, ponder and contemplate not only the animation of a puppet, but also the establishment of one's character?

BIG LEFTY
I don't know about that, Man; I'm just thinking some have it; some don't.

MR. SOCK
Wait a minute. Before you move along with talk about characterization, remember there are a few of us who haven't even been mentioned yet, and it would be appropriate to share the stage, so to speak, and take some time with each of us. Right? So let's do it!

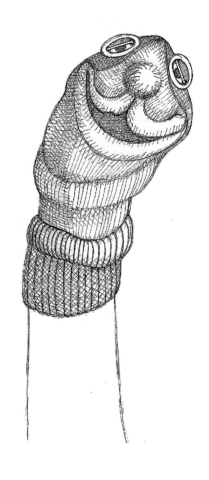

Hanging over there is my very good friend, the internationally recognized marionette. Behind that curtain is a shadow puppet; this one has traveled all the way from Indonesia to be with us. Those little guys are the finger puppets. And I am a sock puppet. Of course, there are lots of others who may be ready to join us later, but for now, I just want to make sure that each of us present gets a moment in the spotlight, and so let's give our courteous attention. Please join me in a round of applause to welcome these noteworthy puppets.

MARIONETTE

Thank you. Thank you. Thank you. I'd like to go first. I've been dangling around and my strings tend to get knotted, if I don't get things straight from the beginning. Thank you. Thank you. Thank you. I'd just like to say that we marionettes are incredibly adaptive, and there is nothing we can't do!!!! For example, both my tail and tongue can be controlled with the correct string.

MADAME SILHOUETTE

My friends, the marionette is no braggart. Indeed, he and his fellows can be manipulated to perform incredible and intricate motions. I will never cease to be amazed by their articulate agilities. I, and those like me, who are dependent on lighting for greatest effect, remain in awe of possibilities. Nevertheless, we are proud that through silhouette, we can tell stories with great detail, action and emotion.

MISS MUFFET
Oh, Madame Silhouette Puppet, please forgive me for interrupting, but I simply have to ask you about your "dependence" on lighting. You see, I need lighting, too, for the sparkle in my eyes, which is so important, because it helps *them* to think I am alive. So, I am wondering, if you are behind a curtain, how can you be . . . well . . . sparkly?

MADAME SILHOUETTE
Ahhh, very fine question. The effect of sparkle comes through cuttings and perforations in our silhouette shapes. We shadow puppets are forms with positive and negative areas, open or not for show of light.

BIG LEFTY
Wow, Dude; I mean, Lady Dude, that is so far out. Like way cool.

MADAME SILHOUETTE
I thank you, Mr. Big Lefty, for your positive regard. And I would like, respectfully, to acknowledge your own straightforward method of communication as simple and yet very effective.

BIG LEFTY
Whoa, Lady Dude. You humble me, Man; I mean, Lady Dude.

FINGER PUPPETS
Okay! Okay! It's our turn! We're the finger puppets. Yeah! We are so small and cute. We don't require big quantities of material for construction, and we're easy to pack 'n' transport because of our size. Let's hear it for "Less is more"! Less is more! Less is more!" Whooop!

It's no kidding that little kids love us because we're tiny. And it's really so fun that one of them can have ten of us acting at the same time. Let's hear it for the finger puppets!!!! Whooop!

MR. SOCK

That was great. Wasn't it folks? And I am truly, so proud to be associated with these artistic and diverse puppet forms. Truly.

Now, I'd like to slow down a bit and take a moment to reflect on experience as a sock puppet, and speak for my fellow sock puppets. We have not always been highly regarded. Throughout the years, many of us have been separated from our partners, or somehow tattered by the ravages of wear or washing machines.

But there is resiliency among sock puppets. And so I'd like to share an anecdote about another sock puppet.

It's a personal and moving—but *true*—story about a sock puppet who is finally achieving incredible acclaim, after an initially stressful and bleak early life. It began as an ordinary, size 9-11 white athletic sock. As was typical for a sock in its time, this normal and practical garment experienced wear, unfit conditions, and frequent washings which included bleach, until it was eventually misshapen, without elasticity, and facing exile in the trash. I think you all have the picture—a dingy, tube of weary cotton without purpose or hope. But there was a day, when one of *them*, who had not yet been inhibited by *human maturity*, and who maintained some creative zest, found this forsaken sock.

Call it luck; consider it a miracle, but using a folded piece of index card for the mouth, secured in place with thread at crude, half-inch stitches, and adorned with black, ball-point-pen ink eyes and nostrils, this lifeless cotton tube was reborn as a sock puppet.
It had been created as a gift, left with a note that read, "See me about this," and subsequently discovered by another one of *them* who has ever since, cherished this humble and astonishing sock puppet. Hopefully, many will read about this incredible sock puppet, and in time the true story of this strong individual will be known throughout even far-away lands.

MISS MUFFET

Oh, my! Oh, my! I am just swirling. A dingy tube of cotton became a puppet! Sparkle through perforations in silhouette shapes can illuminate a story! Some puppets dangle on strings that can get knotted! And finger puppets—all of them, maybe on one hand at the same time can be talking and telling a story! It is so incredible and presents such potential, that I can not help but place my hands together at my right cheek in awe and excitement, and I think I might just swoon into the flounce of my pink, dotted-Swiss skirt. Oh, my! Oh!

SPIDER

Excuse me, Miss. I just want you to know that if you do faint or something, I'll be real close by on the stage, and one of my eight legs can catch you before your beautiful blue hair even touches the floor. You'll be okay. No matter how excited you get hearing about different kinds of puppets, or the intensity of light sparkling from your lovely, expressive eyes, you'll be safe. Isn't that right, Big Lefty? Because we will be here for you.

BIG LEFTY

Yeah, sure. I may just look like a hand at the end of somebody's arm. But when a lady puppet faints on stage, I know what to do. You'll be okay, because I know mouth-to-mouth resuscitation. So, if you do lose it, our leggy friend will keep you from falling off the stage, and I'll keep you sparkly, even if the stage lights go out. No problemo.

MISS MUFFET

Oh, well that is comforting. Thank you, Spider. I hope you do not mind if I call you, Spider? And Mr. Lefty, thank you for your willingness.

SPIDER

Ah, gee, Miss. I'm happy to hear a sweet voice like yours say, "Spider" and if you need me, I'll try real hard to not trip myself getting to you, or to stick a foot in my mouth when speaking, in response, to what ever lovely thing it was that you said.

BIG LEFTY

No problemo.

CHAPTER 2

Why Puppets?

PROFESSOR
And THAT, will be enough! It is clearly time to move on with further explanation, lest we diminish our endeavor entirely to insignificant puppet conversation. I propose that we review what has been clearly established thus far, through what at times has been rather interesting dialogue. So, to be succinct regarding puppets, they are small-scaled figures whose acts are controlled by an outside force or influence, such as the hand, and there have been and are many different puppet forms.

A question, then, about which to wonder, ponder, and indeed, contemplate, is why? *Why* would one outside force use a small-scale figure to do something? Notice now how I am scratching my head, a gesture indicating that I am wondering, pondering and contemplating. And I certainly encourage you to do so, and to repeat after me, "Why? Why? Why?"

FINGER PUPPETS

We know! We know! Let us say why!!!
Puppets are F U N! Puppets are F U N!

P L A Y matters! P L A Y matters!

PROFESSOR

Bravo to you finger puppets, for you have indeed identified a significant reason for the existence of puppets and the occurrence of their manipulations. I will restate, if I may. Put simply, for *fun*. Fun. Funny fun. Tee Hee fun. For, you see, fun stimulates feel-good chemistry in the brain. And play certainly does matter. Indeed, all creatures—even animals without a neocortex—enjoy play. In fact, I recently read Dr. Temple Grandin's best-selling book, <u>Animals in Translation</u> (2005), in which on pages 93 through 124 it is explained that the "emotion of joy" comes from "play circuits in the brain" (p 118). Be it physical play . . .

MISS MUFFET

Oh, like swirling?

PROFESSOR

Yes, even swirling. As I was about to say, whether one's fun is physical, social or with an object, play promotes physical development, coordination, social understanding, and skills. Furthermore, there are researchers who theorize that play teaches young creatures how to handle novelty and surprise.

MS. UP

YOO HOO! It's me again! Over here! I heard the word *surprise*, which is my cue to pop up. So I did, and reeeeally fast, even without help. Weren't you surprised? And you just never will know when I might do it again.

BIG LEFTY

Geeze, Man; not to disrespect, but Dude, you asked why do stuff with a puppet; that's a no brainer. It's like a cool way to communicate, Man. I might like totally zone out with a lecture or some other boring stuff, nothing personal, Dude. But if a chick with blue hair and sparkly eyes, or a bud with lotsa hairy legs, or an old cotton tube with a folded piece of index card for a mouth has the stage, I'm gonna notice. And if I notice something that's interesting, instead of B O R I N G, again, no offense, Man, I'm gonna like pay attention. And if I pay attention long enough, I might learn something. And if it's way interesting, I might even remember it. If it's totally cool, I might even think about it later, and get my own idea. I might even get an idea that's like totally new, Man; something nobody has ever thought of before. And I might get so into my totally brand new idea that I'll wanta do something with it, because it's so interesting. And I'll start to think, "Wow! I must be a genius!" And I'll get so jazzed that I'll wanta share my genius idea with somebody. And that dude will really go wild about my totally new thing, and think that I'm like a way genius, instead of just a hand; so geeeze, Man, that's why.

PROFESSOR
I see, Mr. Lefty. You are suggesting that *use* of an object as a *puppet* to present content, is perhaps more effective than lecture, as *manipulations* may interest and even engage an observer.

BIG LEFTY
Like I said, Man; it's a no brainer.

MISS MUFFET
Hmm. Humm. Excuse me; may I say something? Well, after I did not swoon, I went back to listening, and then I began thinking about *why*, like the professor suggested.

So, adding on to what Mr. Lefty said, well, actually I have two thoughts. First, when I notice someone who is trying to tell something, I get truly interested . . . from my heart.

While I am watching the gestures and listening to what is being said, I begin to understand what that someone has been experiencing, or is worried about in the future. What I am trying to say is that when I notice someone who is alive, with lots of hairy legs and nice manners, or maybe he has a very strong jaw, or a special way of scratching his head; well, I find myself feeling a little bit connected with that someone who is trying to tell something, and I totally stop thinking about whether my blue hair looks nice, or if there are rumples in my pink, dotted-Swiss skirt. Instead, I find myself feeling—what I think—the others must be feeling.

PROFESSOR

Excellent, Miss Muffet. You have identified a social awareness called *empathy*, which means that you have the capacity to participate in another's feelings or thoughts.

MISS MUFFET

Oh, well, perhaps. May I give an example? Remember the little play, *How to Make a Puppet*. You know how the second hand was lifeless at first, but then slipped on that simple fabric costume. I could somehow feel the thrill of it!!!! It was not dotted Swiss, but it was fabric! However, then, when the puppet realized he did not have a head, it was so disappointing. And later, when one of the eyeballs fell off, and rolled from the stage to the audience. Oh, how very embarrassing that must have been. Truly, I was so caught up in what was happening with those two characters, I did not give even a thought to my hair or my skirt. And, I just felt so pleased for the hand and puppet when their little play had its happy ending.

PROFESSOR

Excellent, Miss Muffet. Your elaboration has helped to clarify the construct *empathy*, which, as I stated, is the ability to feel for another, or walk a mile in his shoes, so to speak. And in thus doing, you have provided another reason as to *why* one outside force would use a small-scale figure to do something. It might indeed be done to assist an audience with feeling for others, and thereby developing empathy.

MISS MUFFET

Oh, well; I have one more thing I would still like to say, if I may. Hmm. Hmm. To me, it seems there is something *safe* about letting someone else, like a puppet, do your talking and express what is really on you mind. As just kind of an example, when Mr. Lefty said, "B O R I N G," it was like he gave his voice to my thought, but no one could blame me for saying something was boring, because Mr. Lefty was the one talking. So, when you think about it, I could say, "I love you," or, "I am really afraid," or, "I do not understand anything that is going on in this environment and that is very scary," with a puppet doing the talking, and no one would suspect that—really—it was me who was having those feelings or thoughts. I would be safe.

PROFESSOR
Indeed, safety; it is a primary drive for all creatures. Furthermore, when one feels *unsafe*, there is inhibition and overall lack of progress. Creatures must feel some degree of safety to take action, perhaps try something new, and learn from novel experience. Professionals in the field of education call this *positive risk taking*.

BIG LEFTY
Hey, I have a friend who's a teacher!

PROFESSOR
Astonishing.

BIG LEFTY
Yeah, Man; I do, and I've been to schools with her a lot, Man. She's swell. She teaches all kinds of kids: little kids, even grown ups, kids who are like way creative, and a lot of 'em with challenges, Man. It can be rough being a kid now days.

PROFESSOR
I dare say. In what ways might that be?

BIG LEFTY
Well, my friend, the teacher says that some kids are like afraid all the time, Dude. School can be a pretty scary place. Like you might not fit in with the rest of the bubbas. There might be bullies at recess, or in the guys' room, or when you're trying to get home, Man. And school stuff can be real hard to do, or get right. Other kids'll snicker, right up in your face, Man. And you might lose your recess. Or you might not have lunch money, or some creep might like steal your lunch and toss it to his bubbas so they can play keep away with your food, Man. And some kids have moms and dads who speak another language when they're at home, and so it's like way hard for those kids to understand the teacher, 'cause it sounds like she's talking a foreign language, Man. There's lotsa scary stuff about school, Dude.

PROFESSOR
I dare say.

BIG LEFTY
Yeah, Man. And my friend, the teacher says sometimes she's even scary to a kid, although she's totally cool. But that's why she brings me along, because kids might not feel safe enough to take a risk—like her exact words, Man—to take a risk and talk to her. But they will always talk to me. They're like, "Big Lefty! Big Lefty!" They want to tell me stuff and show me things they've done. And if I say, "Put your name on your paper," they'll do it, Dude. Course, I use a real polite voice when I tell 'em to do it.

PROFESSOR
So then, Mr. Lefty, and fellows, some outside force might use a small-scale figure in a puppet-like way, not only to promote the development of empathy, but also to help observers feel adequately safe, such that they might engage in positive, risk-taking behaviors.

SPIDER
I'm thinking of another reason why, and it has to do with being shy, and not having much confidence. I know about this from personal experience. You see, once upon a time, I was shy and didn't have any confidence in myself, because, if I **WAS** noticed, others would gasp or shriek, and even try to hit me with a shoe. Some would be nice and stand up for me, and try to protect me by trapping me in a jar, and then letting me go loose outside. But it was obvious that nobody wanted me around, which accounted for my shyness and lack of confidence. I used to hide a lot in pretty boring places, like wood piles, so I wouldn't be noticed and have to deal with shrieking or shoes. Now, you might not believe what I'm going to tell next. It might seem like pure fantasy, but if you would please just be willing to suspend your disbelief for a while, I think you'll be able to understand the point I'm about to make. So, please bear with me.

MISS MUFFET
Oh, Spider. You asked so nicely. Of course I am willing to suspend my disbelief for you.

SPIDER
Thank you, Miss. Okay; here goes. One day, I found this blue hat. It wasn't a small-scale figure like a person or an animal; it was a derby. It was a fine quality, wool derby, with no moth holes, and it was clean, but all by itself, just being there, it wasn't much good for anything. It was just an object. Now, we're getting close to the part when I very first begin to get over my shyness and gain some confidence. It began the moment I noticed that blue derby, and it captured my attention. Of course, before moving toward it, I was still careful to check that no one else was around, so that I felt safe. There wasn't, and I did. Almost like magic, somehow on that day I found my derby, I felt safe enough to take a risk. So I mustered up what little courage I had, and next thing I knew, I became an outside force, influencing a fine, blue derby. I tried it on for size, and looked at the reflection in a nearby window. And I've seen myself in a whole new light since then. It may seem silly, but really, I think it was meant to be. My derby is no longer just an object, I'm no longer shy, and together we are confident that when it's a proper time, like when a lady's present, we'll know what to do. And the point I am trying to make is that something simple can motivate you to do one little thing that may change your whole life.

MS. UP
YOO HOO! Here I am again. I bet you're going to be reeeeally surprised when I tell you that I used to be shy. But it's totally true. I used to be too shy to pop up, even though that was my design. Reeeeally, I used to just move up a teeny bit at a time, because I was so afraid that I didn't know how to pop up the right way. But when I watched others, they were popping up without a care in the world, as if they were playing, and everyone loved it. Then one time I just got caught in the excitement and popped up perfectly, and it was terrific. So I tried it again, and again; my popping up kept improving, and now I'm really good at it, and I'm an expert at surprising!!

SNAPPY
Deet Deet Deet Deet Deet Deet
Accurate N. Concise, here, on location at Busy Elementary School, in Bigtown, Oregon, where everyone works hard so all students will meet national academic standards. When I arrived at BES, the principal told me they serve a population of students among whom there are more than twenty languages spoken at home, and that 90% of BES students are learning English as a second, or even third language.

With me this afternoon is the American Council of Parents and Students' 2010 recipient of the SWELL award, veteran teacher, Mrs. Kiddie Smartandready. Congratulations, Mrs. Smartandready, on being recognized for your great achievements with students.

MRS. SMARTANDREADY
Thank you, Mr. Concise.

:-) **SWELL** (-:

The American Council of Parents and Students

Honors

Mrs. Kiddie Smartandready
from Busy Elementary School
Bigtown, Oregon
as the 2010

Super Wonderful Evidence of Language Learning
Award Recipient

SNAPPY

Some of our viewers may not know that only one teacher in the country is selected annually to receive the SWELL award, based on Super Wonderful Evidence of Language Learning by students. Mrs. Smartandready, please tell our audience, to what do you attribute your students' great success as English language learners?

MRS. SMARTANDREADY

Well, Mr. Concise, my family immigrated to the U.S. when I was elementary school age, and I, myself, learned English as a second language. Luckily, I felt very welcomed in my new American school, and so it was easy to pick up the social language, or what we teachers call, *Basic Interpersonal Communication Skills*; things like, "Hello; will you play with me?" Learning vocabulary related to academic procedures and content was not as simple. Fortunately, I had some wonderful teachers, who knew how to help students like me, who were feeling stressed about trying to learn a new language, at the same time they were learning academic content. In those days, teachers weren't as pressured by scripted curriculum, standardized testing, and the possibility of *merit pay*. They were free to present lessons in whatever ways students could understand. My teachers helped me develop, what educators call, *Cognitive Academic Language Proficiency*. I try to follow the models of those teachers, even though, in today's schools, there seems to be less and less time available for what truly matters to children. My years of teaching experience have taught me that playful, social and creative activities matter to youngsters. And in my opinion, having puppets available during free time, and integrating puppetry into lessons, helps students develop both their *BICS* and *CALPS*.

SNAPPY

Well, as the 2010 SWELL award recipient, your opinion is worth noting, Mrs. Smartandready. Congratulations again, and thank you for speaking with me today.

And now, back to you, within the pages of *The Puppet Explained*.

BIG LEFTY
That Mrs. Smartandready lady reminds me of my friend who's the teacher. Maybe they even know each other, or something. Oh, and like I've got another idea, Man, about why do something puppety with an inanimate object. It's like being creative, Man. My friend who's the teacher says she loves being creative, Man, because the kids she teaches like WAY love it. But I was also remembering this guy I know who thinks he's a rod puppet, the wooden-spoon dude with eyes and arms. I guess he sometimes might wanta be creative, Man; it's just the dude's had a way dull life, Man, and so he's like all business. Mosta the time he's like laying flat on his back in a drawer, which is like closed. He hardly ever even gets out into the light, except when he's being used, Man, and then his head is stuck in some glop getting stirred. I'm starting to feel sad for the dude, Man. Like what chance does he have? He's either flat in some utility drawer, or upside down in a bowl, or drenched in a dish washer. How's he ever gonna get around to being to creative, Man?

PROFESSOR
Interesting and remarkable, Mr. Lefty. I believe that you were actually engaging in critical thinking. Specifically, you were *analyzing perspectives*, which has been explained by the sage educational theorist, Dr. Robert Marzano, as complex analysis done when one has identified different perspectives regarding a topic, and considers the reasoning or logic behind them. Certainly, Mrs. Smartandready may be a creative person, because she's had the benefits of a liberal education, and her attempts at creativity have been reinforced by youngsters whom she teaches; whereas this wooden-spoon fellow has had different and limited experiences. And I do find it remarkable and somewhat amusing, Mr. Lefty, that you are capable of thinking critically. Perhaps there is more to you than meets the eye.

BIG LEFTY
No way, Man. What you see is what you get.

MISS MUFFET
Hmm. Hmm. Excuse me; I would like to say something about being creative, and that is, I believe it is important. If it was not for being creative, we would all be exactly the same. We could all be paper bag puppets with construction paper parts that have been traced, cut out and glued in place. That is not a nice thought. Eeeew. Imagine a world of paper bag puppets all talking just the same way by opening and shutting their mouths along a fold. It simply makes me shiver.

SPIDER
Oh, a paper bag puppet could never compare to you, Miss. Why would anyone look at a bag puppet, if you were there? You're so interesting, unique and captivating.

BIG LEFTY
Well, an audience might not get into looking at a bunch of bag puppets, Man, but I've seen a LOT of them, 'cause they're like really easy to make, Man, and like cheap, you know.

MR. SOCK
Wait a minute. Before you talk about supplies, costs, and being frugal, remember there are others of us who can be made without much expense. I'm simply a sock for the most part. And think of the finger puppets; they don't take much by means of materials. And what about the junque puppets? They can be made from anything! Reduce, reuse, recycle when making a junque puppet. What's better than that?

MISS MUFFET
Hmm. Hmm. I would like to say something more about being creative, and that is, when you are different, you are noticed as an individual. Others will take time to look at you, and listen to what you are saying. They can not just react to you as a stock-character stereotype.

PROFESSOR
An astute observation, Miss Muffet. And I will elaborate, based on multiple, previous conversations with a colleague, who just so

happens to teach children's literature courses at the university level. This professor chooses to spark her students' creativity through a writing assignment, which begins with individuals creating their own junque puppets. Ad hoc, she has noted that students who feign making a puppet, and instead write about a standard character, say a boy, or horse, or cat, composing characterizations that tend to be flat, as there is presumed understanding about what constitutes "boy" ness, or "horse", etc. On the other hand, my colleague has found that written descriptions of junque puppets are unusually detailed, fresh, and intriguing. She has concluded that physically constructing a character that is completely novel is stimulating for her students, and as a result they are eager to introduce their unique puppets, think about words that are truly descriptive, and produce writing worth reading.

MADAME SILHOUETTE
Friends, my admiration goes to professor who found way of helping her mature students rekindle creativity. Too often, many persons are discouraged by imperfections in creative attempts and relinquish hope of bringing into being novel idea or form. And are many persons not, these days, fortified by conformity?

BIG LEFTY
Wow, Lady Dude, I'm into your wiseness. I like hang on your words, Man; I mean, Lady Dude. But see, I'm thinking the problem is, most dudes are like really lame at being creative. They like reach a certain point, and then Dah Ta Dah!!!!, being creative is like over, Man, I mean Lady Dude.

MADAME SILHOUETTE
Ahhh; then all more important that creativity be nurtured among young ones. Do we agree?

BIG LEFTY
Yeah, Lady Dude, but how's it gonna happen? Without like really special people—who are still turned on by stuff—teaching creativity to other dudes? Or creativity is like doomed, Lady Dude.

MADAME SILHOUETTE

There is saying, *If you believe thing to be so, and act in accordance, consequences are real.* I believe creativity resides in us all. And I believe it is important to maintain sparks of creativity. I do act accordingly. Others, too, believe in nurturing creativity and act in accordance; many others, and so creativity shall not be doomed.

BIG LEFTY

That'd be cool, Lady Dude, if creativity could manage to not be doomed after all. Maybe I've been like on the verge of being fortified by conformity or something. Whoooa; that was close, because I do really dig what Miss Muffet said about being different getting you noticed as an individual. Like remember the first time I saw Snappy? I like *had* to notice the dude; he'd like stick out in a giant crowd of bag and spoon dudes. I was like instantly grabbed by Snappy's uniqueness and then BAM! got curious about what he'd wanta say.

MISS MUFFET

Yes. It was thrilling. I will always remember meeting Snappy. He is such an individual.

PROFESSOR

Madame Silhouette Puppet and others, please permit me to summarize significant concepts in the preceding dialogue. We had posed a question. *Why* would one outside force use a small-scale figure to do something? Our wondering, pondering and contemplating began with the notion that fun—Tee Hee fun—stimulates beneficial brain chemistry and development. It was mentioned that as methodology for generating fun, non-threatening communication and play via puppetry can cause persons to take notice, attend and engage, which then potentially improves retention of communications, provokes new ideas, fosters empathy, supports positive risk taking, increases confidence, and encourages creativity, all of which facilitates social and academic learning.

SNAPPY

Accurate N. Concise, here, speaking live from pages of *The Puppet Explained*, where the Professor has just summarized recent dialogue among puppets. Let's hear what others have to say, beginning with Madame Silhouette Puppet.

MADAME SILHOUETTE
Ahhh. I am humble in presence of Professor, who has impressive credentials and speaks authoritatively.

SNAPPY
Thank you, Madame Silhouette Puppet. Big Lefty, what's your reaction.

BIG LEFTY
Well, Man, the dude got us thinking, like deeply, Man.

SNAPPY
And Miss Muffet, let's hear from you.

MISS MUFFET
Oh, my! I just love wondering, pondering and contemplating. It is so exciting. And when we talked about being creative, I truly felt like swirling.

SNAPPY
Thank you, Miss Muffet. Spider, what's your take on this?

SPIDER
I think feeling safe is important. And I also think being courteous and helpful are important.

SNAPPY
Many folks would agree with you, Spider. We have time for one more. Mr. Spoon, what would you like to tell the audience?

MR. THE SPOON
Sometimes less is more.

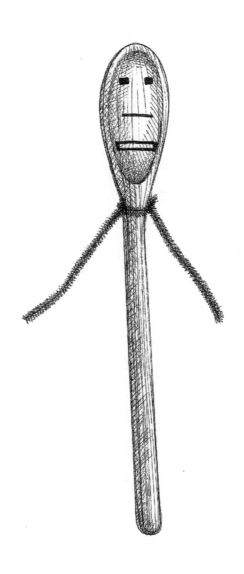

SNAPPY

There you have it. Unrehearsed comments from regular puppets. I'm Accurate N. Concise, and it's back to you.

CHAPTER 3

Does It Matter
Where They Are?

BIG LEFTY
Back to you like where, Man? I'm like looking all around, Man, and here we are and it's back to us, but where in the world are we?

SPIDER
Well, I know where we're not. We're not in a boring place like a wood pile. I've spent too much time in a wood pile, and I'd rather not be there again.

BIG LEFTY
But Spider, Dude; think about it, Man. How do you know we're not in a wood pile?

SPIDER
Well, I might be a spider, but I do have my five senses. Nothing here *looks* like a wood pile. It doesn't have that damp woody *smell*. There's nothing that *feels* hard or splintery where we are. I haven't heard any *sounds* or *tasted* anything that would make me think this place is a wood pile. I do trust my senses a lot when it comes to knowing where I am, and this place is not a wood pile.

BIG LEFTY
Okay, okay, Dude, so we're not hangin' at a wood pile. But so, like where *are* we?

MISS MUFFET
Hmm. Hmm. I am wondering, Mr. Lefty, does it really matter where we are, as long as we are puppets and together? I am thinking back to the play, *How to Make a Puppet*. It had two characters and a fun little story with a sweet ending. Still there was not any setting for the play, not even a curtain as backdrop. Truly, that play could have happened anywhere.

MR. SOCK
I'd like to take the floor for a moment, if no one objects. I'm thinking that it's definitely important to know where we are. It has huge impact; at least that's been the case for many of my sock puppet acquaintances in the stories they've told me. Imagine being stuffed inside a shoe all day. Of course, it is nice when folded up neatly with your mate, and snug inside a closed drawer, but when the setting changes, not-so-nice things can happen. Socks can get separated. Some make it into a laundry hamper, but others don't. And, do you have any idea . . . what it's like inside a hamper? Have you thought about who else might be in there? There are kitchen towels who've been rung so tight that they dry that way. And burp cloths caked with spit up. And undergarments who have been exposed to . . . well, I won't say. And the hamper's only one place.

The washer's worse. If you're tossed in there, you'd better be able to hold your breath for a long time, because when it floods, there is no higher ground. And with all the detergent, you can't see for bubbles. But it's agitation that's really wearing. You're pushed around, and can't possibly get your bearing. You've absolutely no control during agitation; you have to just go with it and hope for the best. And by the spin cycle, you're exhausted and limp.

I'm not trying to shock anyone, and certainly wouldn't want to make you swoon, Miss Muffet, but I firmly believe in knowing about where you are at all times.

MISS MUFFET
It is quite all right, Mr. Sock. You are sharing important information. In my sheltered life, surroundings have hardly been mentioned,

except that there is always a tuffet wherever I happen to be. It is probably time that I begin to think about settings and how they can affect us, so please go on with your examples.

MR. SOCK

I'll give just one more, the drier, because if you can make it through a drier, there's a chance things can work out for you. The drier's a place a lot like a washer, but without water and agitation, which is good. What's bad is that it's a super sauna. Heat beats at you from the drier's entire cylinder, and you will sweat until you're parched. If you're lucky, one of *them* will let you out before wrinkles set, and you might even get matched again with your mate. But if not, every second that you're waiting wrinkles get deeper and stronger, and without moisture you're completely defenseless. So you may be doomed to another cycle. Some items even get ironed. Thank goodness, that seldom happens for socks. Most socks make it.

MISS MUFFET

Oh, my. My. Oh, my. I now understand what you mean about surroundings having an impact. That was certainly clear in examples about your acquaintances. Yet, on the other hand, we have absolutely no idea where we are and all of us are just fine.

BIG LEFTY

Whoa, Dude; I mean, Miss. I've been contemplating this stuff since Snappy gave it back, and I've got a bottom line, which is—we know exactly where we are, and that's like nowhere, which can be cool for some puppet dudes, 'cause it has like nothing to do with what's happening while we're here. But for other dudes, where they are, Man, is it. Like the *where* can be a problem, Dude, and be the whole deal.

PROFESSOR

Mr. Lefty, if I deciphered your comment correctly, you have suggested that the environment or "setting", as I shall call it, may or may not impose a problem or become a source of conflict for characters. Is that a reasonable restatement of your *bottom line*?

BIG LEFTY
I guess so, Man. I was like completely okay with being nowhere until—BAM!—it hit me; we're like nowhere. But for other dudes, like Sock's bubbas, like where you are can be a major problemo.

So now I'm thinking back to hangin' with my friend who's a teacher.

SPIDER
Well, your teacher friend is probably always in a school. That would be a safe place. People are courteous and helpful when they are in a school.

BIG LEFTY
I wasn't thinkin' about being safe, Man. I was rememberin' stuff she's done with her kids when I've been hangin' out with her. Like this one time she showed 'em a bunch of posters.

MISS MUFFET
Oh, I am so interested in hearing about your teacher friend and the children. What was on the posters?

BIG LEFTY
Whoa, come to think of it, it was like YOU! You and Spider!

SPIDER
Are you kidding? Are you pulling my legs? Your teacher friend showed her kids posters with Miss Muffet and me? That's amazing. I took a risk and left the wood pile, found a blue derby and tried it on, practiced tipping the derby politely so I could do it nicely and with confidence in the presence of a lady, and you saw me on a poster with Miss Muffet. Gee Wiz! That's amazing!

BIG LEFTY
Slow it, Man. It's not like that, Man.

MISS MUFFET
It is rather surprising that your teacher friend would have posters showing Spider and me. How did she get them?

MS. UP
YOO HOO! Here I am again. I heard my cue!

SPIDER
Oh, Ms. Up. Nice to see you. Where have you been?

MS. UP
Silly me, I don't know. Where have I been? Maybe I was nowhere. But someone said, "Surprise," which is my cue. So, now that I'm here, should I stay a while, or would you rather I pop down again?

MISS MUFFET
Oh, please do stay, Ms. Up. Mr. Lefty was just going to tell us about a time when his teacher friend showed her students posters of Spider and me. Of course, Spider and I had no idea that we were ever on posters, so it is very exciting news. And I was just asking Mr. Lefty about how his teacher friend got the posters.

SNAPPY
Deet Deet Deet Deet Deet Deet
Accurate N. Concise, here, live from pages of *The Puppet Explained*, where a puppet character, Big Lefty has just broken the news that Miss Muffet and Spider were shown together on posters seen by children in a school classroom. For more on this, let's go straight to the source and hear from Big Lefty.

BIG LEFTY
Wait a minute, Snappy, Dude. This is gettin' outta hand, Man.

SNAPPY
But, Big Lefty, you just said that a teacher *showed a bunch of posters* and on them were Miss Muffet and Spider. Now please tell our audience how the teacher got those posters.

BIG LEFTY
How'm I supposed to know, Dude? Probably at some professional workshop or something. Teachers are always sharing stuff, Man.

SNAPPY
Are you saying it's possible that other teachers have these posters and they have been shown to children in other school settings? Possibly in schools throughout the US?

There you have it, Ladies and Gentleman, straight from puppet character, Big Lefty's own lips. There is a possible connection between what we have just heard, and what is happening in schools across America. Yes, there's a worrisome possibility that children are actually being exposed to posters showing Miss Muffet and Spider. Stay tuned for more on this story.

BIG LEFTY
Whoa, Snappy, Dude, Man, slow down before you swallow your microphone with that big mouth of yours and get it stuck in your throat, Man. Outrageous, Dude. Sheeez. And where's the Professor when I need him?

PROFESSOR
I am right here, Mr. Lefty, where I have been this whole time.

BIG LEFTY
Aw, don't go with that again, Dude. That's what got this mess started, Man, bein' nowhere or bein' somewhere.

PROFESSOR
I sense you are feeling a bit agitated, Mr. Lefty, and perhaps frustrated. May I suggest that we reconstruct what just transpired and untangle the current situation?

BIG LEFTY
Allright. You go, Dude. Cool.

PROFESSOR
Thank you, Mr. Lefty. And I recommend that you take a deep breath, as I shall proceed.

BIG LEFTY
Okay, Man, but how long do I hafta hold it?

PROFESSOR
As long as you are comfortable, Mr. Lefty, and then simply let it go.

BIG LEFTY
Okay, Man.

PROFESSOR
Allright, then. You said the teacher showed her students posters. You do not need to respond orally; just nod.

And when asked what was depicted on these posters, you indicated Miss Muffet and our good friend, Spider. Just nod.

Then Spider and Miss Muffet were surprised and intrigued as to how a teacher had obtained such posters, Ms. Up heard her cue, Miss Muffet remarked that the posters were exciting news, and *Snappy* appeared out of nowhere.

BIG LEFTY
PFEEEEEeeeeeeew. I hcld it as long as I could, Man. It just happened again, Man, talkin' about where a character has like, been. That's the whole confusion with dudes here.

PROFESSOR
Now, now, Mr. Lefty; I believe we were making progress with recounting and untangling, so let's continue, and without distracting prattle, about what I shall hence forth refer to as *setting*. Shall we?

BIG LEFTY
Okay, Man. I'm with ya, Man.

PROFESSOR
Splendid. Now, I believe more important than *how* your teacher friend obtained these posters, is the question regarding what exactly was depicted on the posters.

BIG LEFTY
Okay, Man. It was like a circle, a rectangle, a triangle and a big asterisk mark.

PROFESSOR
Excuse me, Mr. Lefty, but I thought you said the posters were of Miss Muffet and this good fellow, Spider.

BIG LEFTY
That's all wrong, Dude. What I said was it was *like* these guys. The posters had just some shapes, Man, and the kids were supposed to look at the shapes and figure out what they were supposed to be; like they represented something.

PROFESSOR
Oh, as a code perhaps?

BIG LEFTY
No, Dude, not a code, but like shapes that represented stuff the teacher wanted her kids to be thinking about, Man. Here, let me show you.

BIG LEFTY

So, my friend the teacher shows her kids these posters so they'll figure them out, Man. And if they don't, she'll explain. Here's what I remember. The circle equaled like a *character*. And as an example, she used Miss Muffet.

MISS MUFFET

Oh, how very touching that she would think of me.

BIG LEFTY

And the rectangle is like where it's happening, Man. Like what you call a *setting*. So the setting is a tuffet, whatever that is.

MISS MUFFET

Well, mine is a low seat, as are most tuffets. Mine is upholstered with lime-time green suede. It is very nice and quite comfortable.

BIG LEFTY

Okay, green suede; okay; yeah. So one poster is like about a *character* in a *setting*. And the next poster shows a triangle next to the circle on the rectangle. And my teacher friend explained that the triangle was like "habitual behavior", Man. That's what she said. And so for the character, Miss Muffet, nothin' personal and no offense, Miss, my teacher friend said it was "eating her curds and whey", whatever that stuff is, which was what the teacher explained was what Miss Muffet usually did.

MISS MUFFET

Oh, my. Well, yes; often I do. You see I get my dairy nutrients through eating curds and whey. I do also eat foods from the other nutrient groups, as it is important to have a well-balanced diet, in order to keep sparkle in my eyes and healthy blue hair.

BIG LEFTY

Okay, so on the next poster there's the character circle, setting rectangle and behavior triangle, and up in the corner is like a big asterisk mark, which my teacher friend said was an "antagonist", which means like a *bad* dude. I'm sorry, Spider, but she said, "spider." I'm sorry, Man; she musta been talkin' about one of your bubbas, Dude; she couldn't have meant you, Man, but she said, "Along came a spider."

SPIDER
Well, it's not the first time, Big Lefty. And I've learned to deal with it. So don't feel bad, Big Lefty. I couldn't hold you responsible for what someone else had said.

BIG LEFTY
Thanks, Spider. That's big of you, Man.

Okay, so the fourth poster shows the circle on the rectangle with the triangle and the asterisk mark is on the rectangle real close to the circle. And my teacher friend said, "And sat down beside her." She told her kids that it showed like a big *conflict* in the story. You know, the like big-deal character real close to the bad-dude character.

MS. UP
Wowie! Zowie! I'm so happy that I didn't go back down. This is the verrrry most interesting time up I've ever had ever. I can hardly wait for what's going to happen next!!

PROFESSOR
Ms. Up, if you would simply recall nursery rhymes you learned during childhood, you would know what will occur.

MS. UP
Golly! Gee! I would if I could, but I can't. So I shan't. And I can hardly wait!!!

BIG LEFTY
Okay, so the next poster showed like half a circle at the edge of the poster, and just the asterisk mark sittin' on the rectangle. My teacher friend said, "And frightened Miss Muffet away," which she called the *climax*. Then the last poster is the asterisk mark all alone, Man, on the rectangle.

MISS MUFFET
Oh, Spider. I am so sorry. Nothing like that ever happened, and I am chagrinned that something so untrue would be told as a nursery rhyme. I can just imagine how you must be feeling, Spider. It is so unfair. And it is no wonder that *they* gasp and shriek and try hitting you with shoes, if *they* have been hearing such things since childhood.

SPIDER
Well, don't worry about it, Miss Muffet. My blue derby has helped a lot. Really.

MISS MUFFET
Oh, my. If I could just change the expression on my face from happy to sad, I certainly would, but I seem to have a perpetual smile. I think I will just have to cover my face with my hands. This whole thing is so very unfair and upsetting.

SPIDER
Still, please don't worry, Miss. Everyone has problems, and they usually make us stronger in the long run. Look at me. Here I am in *The Puppet Explained*, having conversations with a blue-haired lady, who's wearing a pink dotted-Swiss skirt. For me, things couldn't be better.

MISS MUFFET
Oh, Spider. That is so very sweet.

CHAPTER 4

What's Going to Happen Next?

PROFESSOR
Lest we get distracted from the significant discussion about which we *had* been engaged, Mr. Lefty, are we to understand that your teacher friend did not show children posters depicting Miss Muffet and Spider? Is it correct that the posters instead presented representations of fundamental *story elements*? Is it also correct that the teacher helped her students to associate the story elements with aspects of a familiar children's rhyme? And why might this teacher do such a thing?

BIG LEFTY
Professor, Dude, I'm just sayin' what I remember. My teacher friend was tryin' to get her kids to think about *where* stuff happens in a story, Man. She told the kids that sometimes *where* stuff happens can be like an important part of the story.

PROFESSOR
In other words, *setting* can be an important story element?

BIG LEFTY
Practically her exact words, Man. And I've seen her do something that like proves it, Dude. She does this like activity, Man, and I've watched her do it with kids and with grown-up dudes. *They* will

be like crawlin' around on the floor on hands and knees, Man, and then *they* make up stories.

PROFESSOR
Mr. Lefty, I do not understand why your teacher friend would have students crawl on the floor, and I'm certain that your fellow puppets are also confused by that statement. What ever are you telling us?

BIG LEFTY
Oh, Dude, Man, it's like so clear once you see this in action, Man. My teacher friend wants students to think like outside the box, Man. You know how students are usually sittin' in desks, Man, and always lookin' at the same stuff. It's like where *they* are, Man; you know, like the typical setting in a school, Man. So to encourage thinking outside the box, Man, she like got *them* on the floor.

PROFESSOR
That is quiet unusual, and I for one find it hard to believe.

BIG LEFTY
No, really, Dude. This is how she did it. She had a finger puppet for each student. I think *they* like made the puppets, Man, but I wasn't there when that happened. Anyway, Man, the puppets were mice, Man. And mice crawl on the floor. Right? It was like a different perspective; you know? So my teacher friend told her students to act like mice, Man, and explore the classroom looking for things that could be like a problem if you were a mouse, Man. Like it'd be colder on the floor, Man, and there could be really sticky places where a mouse could get stuck. And a shoe would be like really big, if you were a mouse, Man. And there might not be much food on the floor, so a mouse might be hungry enough to eat a crayon, or something poisonous, Dude. Whoa, it'd be a whole different world if you were a mouse on the floor, Man.

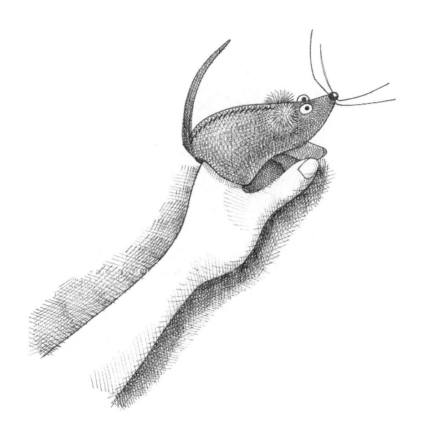

PROFESSOR
Indeed. Well, Mr. Lefty, in my analysis, you have just explained your teacher's approach for *building background*. That is, she structured an activity to make sure all her students had an experience which would prepare them to fully engage in her upcoming lesson on story setting as a source of conflict.

BIG LEFTY
Whatever, Man.

PROFESSOR
Please continue, Mr. Lefty. After building background, what occurred in the lesson?

BIG LEFTY
Okay, Dude. So she had like a worksheet. It like showed the posters I told you about, Dude. Like with the six posters on the left side. Here, let me draw it.

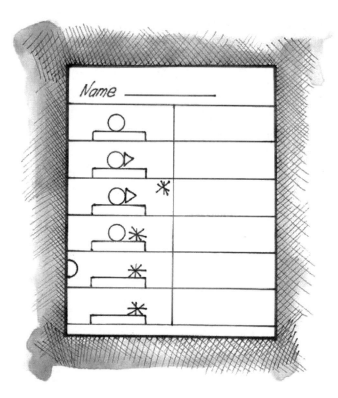

BIG LEFTY
Okay, so the kids or adult dudes were supposed to make up a story, like based on experiences as a mouse. And *they* had to draw the story on this worksheet. My teacher friend said it was okay to use words, Man, but she really wanted dudes to use pictures.

PROFESSOR
I see. Could you provide us with some examples, Mr. Lefty?

BIG LEFTY
Sure, Man. Like in the space next to the circle and rectangle, would be a picture of a mouse on the floor. Dig, it, Dude? And next to the habitual behavior box, like could have been a picture of a mouse thinkin' about food, Man. And in the next space could've been like a crayon, which would've been like the bad-dude, maybe poisonous, antagonist guy. Or like food set in a trap, Dude. Every student drew different stuff on the worksheet, Man, because each one was thinkin', Man, like outside the box. Like think about a mouse whose habitual behavior was like looking for a friend, Man. That'd be a totally different story, Man. Or a mouse who was always being buff, Man. Or a mouse who always wanted to read, Man. Can you see how it'd work, Dude?

PROFESSOR
Yes, Mr. Lefty. And I suspect that your teacher friend had her students use these worksheets in some way. Is that correct?

BIG LEFTY
Well, like *they* shared the stories, Man. She put a worksheet on this like machine that made it like big, Man, so everybody could see it. And then the dude or dudette who drew on the worksheet got to tell bubbas in class about that story, Man. And then bubbas could make like comments, Man, but they had to be school appropriate. You know what I mean, Dude?

PROFESSOR
Regarding *school appropriate*? Most certainly. More so than some others, I might add. At any rate, Mr. Lefty, what you have recounted

is a series of activities that your teacher friend has presented such that her students engaged in thinking outside the box about the story element—setting. It appears that what you have called a *worksheet* served as a pictorial story outline. Do you recall what this teacher did as a culminating activity?

BIG LEFTY

I don't know about culminating, Dude. But I watched what she did next with young kids, Man. She like had the kids pick one worksheet, and then had all the kids sit like really close to her on the floor. But they weren't being mice, Man, they were like sittin' criss-cross applesauce, Man. And she got 'em to like pay attention to this big piece of paper, Man, and she showed the kids how to write that story in like words. She like used big print letters, Man, and had kids give her ideas for what to say, Man. She would have the kids help her spell some words, but she really did like know how to spell, Man, 'cause she's a teacher. She just wanted the kids to show me how smart they were, which was cool, Man, 'cause some words, like *t h e*, Man, you just have to like know. You can't like sound it out, Dude. And like *w a s*, Man; you just hafta like know it. And, Dude, she'd even let one or two kids have a turn writing words, Man, using her big pen. Whoa, the kids thought that was cool, Man. It was like a really big honor, Man, to be chosen to write a word.

SPIDER

Well, it would be! I was just imagining how wonderful it would be sitting with those kids, close to your teacher friend with all my legs criss-cross applesauce. And it would be so wonderful if she chose me to write a word. I would feel so proud if I was selected to use her big pen. Wow, that would be terrific! Just imagine it!

BIG LEFTY

I'm tryin', Spider, Dude, but it's like really hard. How are you gonna like do the criss-cross bit?

PROFESSOR

Mr. Lefty! Let us not get distracted from what you were telling us regarding your teacher friend's lesson about setting as a story element and possible source of conflict. You were just describing how the teacher involved her students with guided practice doing what educators call *shared writing*. Do you recall what came next?

BIG LEFTY

Of course, Man, because I was like helping her with the lesson, Dude. My teacher friend told the kids they were going to write their own stories. And she had me tell the kids who had permission to get up and go to their seats, Man, to get started. I would like let the kids know I was looking for ones who showed me they were like ready. And then I like named a kid or two, and complimented them on walking safely and quietly. I did it just the way my teacher friend would, only my personality is like different than hers. Then I'd like go around the room and compliment kids who were workin' and like real quietly ask some kids to tell me about what they had done so far, you know, Man. I'd like keep 'em focused, encourage 'em, and help out with hard words and like punctuation; you know, Man.

PROFESSOR

I see, Mr. Lefty, you assisted the children with their independent work.

BIG LEFTY

Yeah, Man, as they were like making up their own stories. It was like cool.

Chapter 5

Story Line + Conflict = Plot

MS. UP
YOO HOO! I'm still up over here. And I just realized something that reeeeally came as a surprise to me when I realized it, BUT what I realized is that I have no setting.

SPIDER
Oh, sure you do, Ms. Up. At least I think you have a setting. It's your box, which is with you all the time. Whether you're down inside or popped up and outside, you've got a setting that goes wherever you do, like a turtle has its shell.

MS. UP
Spider, it's reeeeally nice of you to help me try and figure out what I'm realizing. You are so very nice. And you may be right that I do have a setting. But, Spider, I'm still realizing that there's something missing. So if it's not a setting, could maybe it be that I don't . . . have a story? You see, when I'm down inside my box, that's all there is. And when I pop up and am outside my box, that's all there is.

But just now, I popped up and you puppets were talking, and it was so verrrry interesting, and I got caught up in what might happen next, and then, I realized, I've never been part of what's happened next. All I have ever done is to pop up or down. Oh, sure, popping can be different at times. Sometimes I pop up or down reeeeally fast!

Other times I'm slow and cautious, showing a bit at a time and looking side to side suspiciously, or I may POOOF! out of sight. But . . . so . . . reeeeally . . . what has happened . . . other than popping.

SPIDER

Well, Ms. Up, when you said that you don't have a story, did you mean something like a beginning, a middle and an ending? Is that what you meant?

MS. UP

I don't know, Spider. I could have a beginning about popping up, and a middle about while I'm there, and an ending about as I go down again. But does that seem to be . . . enough?

SPIDER

Oh, well, I think I'm beginning to understand. Do you feel like there's no . . .

PROFESSOR

Plot? I wonder if that *might* be Ms. Up's dilemma. She may be concerned that up-ing and down-ing, although they do provide a narrative order, such that this happened first, then the next thing occurred, and subsequently thus and such took place, etc., etc., yet offer no *plot.* Consider, if you will, a description of plot given in the 1992, 3rd edition of Rebecca J. Luken's <u>A Critical Handbook of Children's Literature</u>; it was as follows . . . "possible action and reaction that confronts character, builds the plot." (p 63)

BIG LEFTY

Far out, Man. Like what are you telling us, Dude?

PROFESSOR

Simply that up-ing and down-ing present a limited and redundant narrative order or *story line*, however, up-ing and down-ing alone are not a plot. And, that being said, it may be that Ms. Up's discomfort is actually due to lack of *conflict*.

BIG LEFTY
Whoa, Dude. She's got like the perfect life, Man; a happy-go-lucky, pop-up puppet with like no problemos. How cool is that? So you're like losing me, Man, with this lack of conflict stuff.

PROFESSOR
Understandably, Mr. Lefty, as I have been merely thinking out loud and I have not presented a tidy thesis regarding Ms. Up's lament. Please accept my apology for being less than clear in this situation. And permit me to engage in analysis, which I hope should help to enlighten us all.

BIG LEFTY
Dude. You're gonna like say that a perfectly happy, go-with-the-flow story needs a conflict? Far out, Man.

PROFESSOR
Let us begin with a Premise #1, that conflict in a story provides tension and interest, and without conflict, a story line is predictable. With Premise # 1 in mind, as per Ms. Up, typically she hears her cue and pops up, and then when no longer presenting an element of surprise, she typically returns to a down position within her setting, thus affecting an initial response of surprise, but no genuine tension or reason for interest; no plot.

MS. UP
YOO HOO! Excuse me, Professor. This might seem slightly up-side down for me to say, but I'm actually sad right now because I think you're right. I think I've been a lot of *up* with no real *interest*. And I think that's what reeeeally came as a surprise to me when I realized it.

PROFESSOR
Ms. Up, you must not take this realization as a personal shortcoming. You, Ms. Up, are a puppet, whose acts are controlled by an outside force or influence. And while you are accomplished at what you are expected to do--up-ing and down-ing, your actions and even prescribed speeds, are dictated by a narrative order. And if that

story line lacks conflict, tension or interest, as asserted in Premise #1, you cannot possibly be faulted for predictable behavior, which eventually would be less than interesting.

MS. UP
Oh; golly.

PROFESSOR
So let us engage in further analysis of this situation. What we know is that a character, Ms. Up has a setting, yet feels less than satisfied as activities of the, dare I say, weak story lines in which she has been engaged, have been without conflict, tension and interest.

MADAME SILHOUETTE
Ah. Professor, your perception is keen. Myself, a shadow puppet, illuminating story would be nothing without powerful and clear conflict. My movements would be only play of light and dark, not interesting, without problem to be addressed.

MR. SOCK
Mind if I jump in here, in support of what Madame Silhouette Puppet just said? I'd like to share what I've learned from many of my sock puppet acquaintances through stories they've told me. Unlike socks, that lie in drawers or stretch around feet, sock puppets are truly made to take on problems; it's the actual reason why sock puppets are so very interesting!

MR. THE SPOON
As a spoon, I have been in a drawer a lot. Not much happens.

MISS MUFFET
Hmm. Hmm. I wonder, Ms. Up, has up-ing and down-ing become such a routine, that, well perhaps you are thinking a bit of conflict in your life would be somewhat interesting?

MS. UP
Golly, I don't know, Miss Muffet.

PROFESSOR
I suggest that we consider the addition of conflict to Ms. Up's apparently routine existence. Indeed, let us think about possibilities. Perhaps there could be a scenario in which Ms. Up is motivated to pop up. Perhaps she's prepared to attend the *Puppet Creators' Convention* held each spring in Zannyville. Attending the convention would be an *action*. Such a story line could begin with Ms. Up excited about the PCC and preparing to go. Still, there could be multiple sources of conflict that might interfere. For instance, Ms. Up could be without the assistance of someone to push her rod upward when it's time to check in at an airline's desk, such that she might remain in her box, with airline personnel *reacting* as if Ms. Up was luggage, and to worsen matters, mistakenly route her to a wrong destination, until eventually the problem is discovered and Ms. Up is rerouted. And there is a *plot*. Would such be interesting and possibly satisfying, Ms. Up?

MS. UP
Oh; golly.

PROFESSOR
Or, as another scenario, Ms. Up could arrive safely in Zannyville, which would constitute an *action*, but let's say that many residents of Zannyville are impacted by germs or a virus to which Ms. Up has no immunity, and she becomes so ill, that she is initially hospitalized, which would be a *reaction*, until her innate stamina wins out and she regains sufficient health for pursuing her course to attend the PCC. It's a second plausible plot. Interesting or satisfying?

MS. UP
Golly; oh, golly.

PROFESSOR
Or, as in a romantic plot, Ms. Up could be enraptured—an action—with a charming con puppet, who undermines her strong rod-puppet nature, and entices Ms. Up to join a troop of marionettes—a reaction—only to find that strings are attached,

and yet Ms. Up manages to work her way free from cumbersome entanglements. And you see, yet a third conceivable plot.

MS. UP
Golly; oh, golly oh gee, Professor. Do you mean that just because I have always had the same setting, with up-ing and down-ing as my routine, do you mean that doesn't stop me from having an interesting plot—or two—in my life?

PROFESSOR
Why, Ms. Up, let me assure you that plot is not only possible in your life, it is as probable as sunrise and taxes. Just be open, Ms. Up, to possibilities and begin to recognize plots as they may unfold.

MS. UP
Golly, Gee!!! I will. I will be open to possibilities and look for interesting plots wherever I might be.

PROFESSOR
That is the spirit, Ms. Up!!! And BRAVO! Because, on occasions a character, such as you, or, for that matter, any other of our puppet fellows might weaken during such a personal conflict, and resign herself to what has always been. However, recalling the prophesy told by Madame Silhouette Puppet, *if you believe a thing to be so and act in accordance the consequences are real*, if, believing that you are doomed to a life of routine up-ing and down-ing, you acted accordingly, you would be affected by subsequent consequences, which would then ultimately become a narrative order or story line without conflict and interest. But you, Ms. Up are willing to believe that an interesting plot can *be so*, and act in accordance by looking for interesting plots wherever you might be. And the consequences for your actions, Ms. Up, I dare say, will be real.

BIG LEFTY
Dude, that was like totally not understandable, Man. What did you say? Man, put it in like words that a regular puppet can understand, Dude.

PROFESSOR
Indeed, my apology, I was getting ahead with my own thinking, and you are certainly correct; what I said must have been quite unclear for the rest of you. I do apologize.

BIG LEFTY
It's okay, Man, just remember what Mr. Spoon told Snappy.

PROFESSOR
And that was?

BIG LEFTY
Sometimes less is more.

PROFESSOR
Ah; yes. So perhaps a simple equation will clarify. I'll write it for you.

story line + conflict = plot

With that as a visual reminder, permit me to return to the topic of conflict.

PROFESSOR
Conflict, you see, refers to discord or a battle between a *protagonist* or in colloquial terms, a "good guy", if you will, in this case Ms. Up, and an *antagonist* or "a bad guy" or opposing force. So you see, one possible source of conflict could be another person; thus a *person-against-person conflict*.

MS. UP
But, YOO HOO!!! Professor, I don't know anyone who is a bad guy. In fact, I haven't reeeeally even been up enough to reeeeally know anyone, much less to have a conflict with some one.

PROFESSOR
Fine, Ms. Up, that is entirely fine, as there are three other sources of conflict. A second has to do with the protagonist, for example you, Ms. Up, being in conflict with nature. Say, Ms. Up, that your life was negatively impacted by a natural disaster, such as a sudden and terrible storm, or a drought that comes over the land, parching everything and everyone; thus a *person-against-nature conflict*.

MS. UP
But Professor, I'm almost reeeeally sure that I would never be in a conflict with nature. What I mean is, why would I even want to pop up in a storm or a drought? I'm sort of sure I wouldn't. Besides, if there was a natural disaster, everybody else would be too busy with worrying about the disaster to take notice even if I did pop up, which I'm almost reeeeally sure I wouldn't.

PROFESSOR
Fine, then, Ms. Up, consider if you will, a third source of conflict, *person-against society*, in which a protagonist struggles to over come such things as stereotyping, discriminant wrong doing, and oppression by society at large.

MISS MUFFET
Hmm, hmm, Professor, I do not think person-against-society conflict could ever apply to Ms. Up. She is a personification of happy surprise and gaiety. Why, just look at her sweet face.

BIG LEFTY
I like totally agree, with Miss Muffet, Man. Like why would society ever waste time like bein' in conflict with a pop-up puppet, Dude? And like what kind of conflict could there be, Man? A lot of *them* like meetin' in Zannyvile, Man, picketin' the *Puppet Creators' Convention* to stop 'em from making more dudettes like Ms. Up, here. I don't think so. And even if *they* did, Man, like how could *they* like oppress a pop-up puppet? Like hold her box lid down? Give up on the like person-against-society angle, Man; it's like way unrealistic.

PROFESSOR
Excellent, my puppet fellows. Through an analysis of Ms. Up's newly realized situation, and a deductive sort of process, we can conclude that the fourth source of conflict is relevant to Ms. Up's current realization. That is person-against-self.

MARIONETTE
Excuse, excuse, excuse me. I'd like to speak now. I've been ha, ha, hanging around through all this without saying anything, but Professor, I'd like to get the concept of person-against-self straight from the beginning. So, if I was to tangle my own strings, I mean intentionally make it so that my movements didn't work, would that be an example of person-against-self conflict?

PROFESSOR
I think it could most certainly be, but others might ponder, "Whatever might cause a marionette to self sabotage in such a manner?"

For you see, person-against-self conflict *could* be far less dramatic than what you related. Indeed, it may simply be that the character must deal with an internal conflict such as clinging to childhood or growing up, or wanting to believe that a friend has not betrayed you when actions have demonstrated otherwise, or, as in Ms. Up's case, a conflict could be tension between the comfort of routine and her desire for something more exciting.

Furthermore, I feel it is prudent to consider one's audience when contemplating conflict in a story. If, for example, your audience would be children, then person-against-self conflicts likely to be experienced by children could be appropriate. However, I will go so far as to recommend that more adult sources of person-against-self conflict be reserved for a mature audience.

MARIONETTE
Okay, then. Okay, then. Okay, then. I've got an idea. Say I tangle my own strings. Say I just haven't learned how to dangle, without getting tangled. That's person-against-self; right? Right? Right?

PROFESSOR
Yes; that would be an example of person-against-self conflict.

MARIONETTE
Okay, then. Okay, then. Okay, then. Another idea. Say I want this bone. Say I swing my paw to get it. Say I accidentally push the bone away. Say my next swing pushes it further.

PROFESSOR
Yes, that would be unintentional, yet person-against-self conflict; you would be deterring yourself from obtaining your goal, which would be acquiring the bone.

MARIONETTE
Okay, then. Okay, then. Okay, then. Say I want to catch a bunny. Say I'm in impetuous pursuit! Say I don't stop to plan a bunny-catching strategy. Say I even tell myself to stop and make a plan, but pay no attention to my own advice, and the bunny gets clean away form me.

PROFESSOR
Most certainly.

MARIONETTE
Okay, then. Okay, then. Okay, then. I think I've got it straight. Person-against-self conflict is getting in your own way. I've got it. Thank you. Thank you. Thank you.

PROFESSOR
That's well and good. So let us return to consideration of Ms. Up's habit, which was routinely popping up, remaining there, and then returning down, and doing the afore mentioned without stopping to consider, until Ms. Up's lament, which provoked recognition of an inner conflict. Therein is a person-against-self conflict situation.

However, Ms. Up declared in our presence that she henceforth intends to *be open regarding possibilities and look—wherever she might be—for plots*. She thereby provided a *denouement* for her own story. That is, from the moment Ms. Up stated, "I will be open to possibilities and look for interesting plots wherever I might be," we knew the resolution to Ms. Up's person-against-self conflict.

FINGER PUPPETS
Yeah, for Ms. Up! Yeah! Let's hear it for Ms. Up! Yeah! She's going to be open to possibilities! Yeah! She's going to look for plots wherever she might be. Yeah, for Ms. Up! Let's hear it for Ms. Up! Right on! You go, Girl!! Whoop! Whoop! Whoop!

SNAPPY
Deet Deet Deet Deet Deet Deet
Accurate N. Concise, here, live from pages of *The Puppet Explained*, where there's a great deal of excitement. It seems a small crowd of finger puppets and other characters has gathered to cheer about a recent a denouement. Let's speak directly with those involved to get the full story.

Big Lefty, what's going on here? What's causing all this excitement?

BIG LEFTY
It's great news, Man!

SNAPPY
That's why I'm here. So, Big Lefty, tell us about this recent denouement.

BIG LEFTY
I don't know about that, Man. It's Ms. Up, Dude. She's like realized an inner conflict like with herself, Man, and has like decided what to do about it, Man.

SNAPPY
That is exciting news. Thank you, Big Lefty.

BIG LEFTY
No problemo, Man.

SNAPPY
Accurate N. Concise, here, about to speak with a crowd of highly excited finger puppets. Let's hear what they have to say.

FINGER PUPPETS
Yeah, for Ms. Up! Yeah! Let's hear it for Ms. Up! Yeah!

SNAPPY
What can you tell us about the denouement?

FINGER PUPPETS
It's all about the denouement. We're cheering to show Ms. Up our support! We're with you, Ms. Up!!! Yeah!! We're happy and with you 100%. Yeah, Ms. Up!!!

SNAPPY
Thanks, folks, and here is the Professor. Let's see what he can tell us about all this.

Professor, we understand there's been a denouement.

PROFESSOR
Yes, you see, one of our fellows, Ms. Up has revealed to us a complex sequence of events, which unbeknownst until recently has been a source of inner conflict. The outcome of which is that Ms. Up has decided to proceed henceforth with a different outlook, the consequences of which will certainly resolve the identified issue.

SNAPPY
Thank you, Professor. That helps to explain all the excitement. Now let's speak directly with Ms. Up, and find out her reaction to what's happening.

Ms. Up! Ms. Up! If I could have a moment with you, Ms. Up. I'm Accurate N. Concise. Ms. Up, would you please tell us, in your own words, about all this excitement.

MS. UP
Oh; golly, Mr. Concise.

SNAPPY
Call me, Snappy.

MS. UP
Oh, alright, Snappy.

SNAPPY
So, again, Ms. Up, in your own words, what's so exciting?

MS. UP
Oh, alright. Golly, it's kind of a reeeeally complex story, because I've always been waiting for my cue and up-ing and down-ing became such a routine but that didn't seem to be enough, and then Spider tried to help me figure out what was wrong, and the Professor said my problem was lack of conflict. And then golly, oh, gee, the Professor said that I could have some conflicts. He suggested problems getting to Zannyville, and lack of immunity, and being distracted by a charming con puppet. And then I decided to believe that I truly could have conflicts and that would mean rather than just up-ing and down-ing, I could have plot. And when I realized that I could have plot, I announced I was going to be open for possibilities and look for plots wherever I might be. Golly, gee, that's reeeeally what started all this excitement. Because at that moment everyone knew how my problem with and up-ing and down-ing not being enough would be resolved. Oh, golly, gee; it's as simple as that and so exciting! And I want to thank all my new friends here

in *The Puppet Explained* for being so supportive. And could I just say hello to my mom and dad? "Hello, Mom!" "Hi, Daddy."

SNAPPY

There you have it, live from pages of *The Puppet Explained*, a lot of excitement about a recent denouement, and some very happy puppets. This has been Accurate N. Concise reporting and now it's back to you.

CHAPTER 6

What's It All Mean?

SPIDER
Back to me?

SNAPPY
Why, sure, Spider. Why not? Back to you.

SPIDER
Oh, okay. So then since it's back to me, would it be alright if I ask a question? It's something I've been wondering about for a while.

MISS MUFFET
Hmm. Hmm. I would like to say something about Spider asking a question, and that is, Spider has always been kind and helpful, so I think the least we can do is to listen attentively when Spider asks his question.

SPIDER
Oh, thank you, Miss. I appreciate that because I've been hesitant about asking, even though I keep wondering.

BIG LEFTY
Aw, come on, Spider, Man. We're all behind ya, Dude. What's the question, Man?

FINGER PUPPETS
Yeah, for Spider! Yeah! Spider's got a question! Let's hear it, Spider! Yeah!

Right on! You go, Spider. We're listening.

SPIDER
Oh, okay; well I've been wondering about something. Well sort of every now and then I find myself leaning on one of my eight legs and scratching my chin with another, because I've been trying to figure out what it all means.

BIG LEFTY
Dude, what do you mean, *what it all means?*

SPIDER
That's what I'm wondering, Big Lefty. What it all means.

BIG LEFTY
Spider, Dude, like what do you mean, *what it all means?* Like *it*, Man. What *it* do you mean? How're we gonna help you with the question, Man, if we don't know what *it* you mean when you ask *what it all means?*

SPIDER
Oh, well, okay; what I guess I'm wondering is *so what?*

BIG LEFTY
Dude, what kind of a question is *so what*, Man? *So what* about *what*, Man?

SPIDER
Well, okay; I'll try and put it another way. What I am wondering is *what does it all mean?* I mean, *so what?*

BIG LEFTY
Whoa, Dude! You're like confusing me, Man. We like need some help here, Man. Like where's the smart Professor dude when we need him?

PROFESSOR
Here, Mr. Lefty. I am right here. Hello to you, Mr. Lefty. And hello, Spider.

BIG LEFTY
Dude.

SPIDER
Hello, Professor. I didn't mean to bother you with my question. It's really not important. It's just something I keep wondering about a lot.

PROFESSOR
Spider, my good fellow, do you recall that while I was introduced early in *The Puppet Explained* I admitted to being somewhat bald? Well, I can tell you with certainty that baldness in my case is not an inherited trait, but rather the result of head scratching, which is a habit that coexists with my tendency to extensively wonder, ponder and contemplate. That being said, Spider, if you have a question that causes *you* to wonder, occasionally and perhaps frequently, then your query is of interest to me. So, Spider, you find yourself wondering about . . .

SPIDER
Well, Professor, I've noticed that we puppets, you know, Miss Muffet, and you, and Big Lefty and the Finger Puppets; well, you know; all of us . . .

PROFESSOR
Yes, there are quite a few of us puppet characters. Yes, go on Spider.

SPIDER
Okay, well, we're all here or at least we're someplace; whether we've noticed or not, we are somewhere.

PROFESSOR
Yes, Spider, we characters are in a setting, which may be important to a story, or merely a backdrop, yet we do exist in some setting.

SPIDER
That's what I've been thinking about, Professor. And then things happen. Actually, there's usually a story with some sort of beginning, middle and ending.

PROFESSOR
Ah, narrative order. Yes, Spider. But remember that narrative order without conflict does not equal plot.

SPIDER

Oh, well, I have remembered that, Professor. And actually it was about when Ms. Up realized that up-ing and down-ing might not be enough, and you suggested that she actually could have plot, or actually several plots in her life, that's about when I found myself wondering what it all means. And now I keep wondering; *so what*?

PROFESSOR

Ah, Spider. I think I'm beginning to comprehend your consternation. I think you may be grappling with the concept of *theme*, and that, good Spider is quite understandable. For, certainly there may be charming characters and elaborate settings where complicated plots unfold, and yet, no *theme* from which one might gain an insight or learn a universal truth. There may have been a delightful romp, but of no significance. Thus, there was nothing to take away; there was no *theme*.

Let us take a step back, Spider and clarify the word *theme*. It comes from the Greek and it literally means something *laid down*. Something laid down that you, Spider, find significant and memorable, and something you can take away. Without theme one is left to wonder *what does it all mean*? Or as you summarized, *so what*?

SPIDER

Oh, Professor. I think you understand what I've been wondering about in my mind, and I feel better already. Because, you see, while I kept wondering and wondering, I was feeling a bit lonesome that I was wondering all by myself. Then I started getting a bit worried that I was the only one who was wondering what it all means. But now that you said I could have been wondering about a *theme*, I know there's a word for what I've been wondering, which makes me think that others may have wondered this way, too. So it's not just me, wondering for no reason. Perhaps even the Greeks wondered about what it all means. Maybe they wondered so much that they talked to other Greeks, until they came up with a term. Then when one Greek said the word *theme*, other Greeks understood that the first person was wondering about what it all means.

PROFESSOR
My, my, Spider; you are a bright fellow.

SPIDER
Ah. Well. I do feel better knowing I'm not the only, or the first creature to wonder about *what it all means*. And *"So what?"* And it's actually good to know that others have thought about *theme*. But . . . it's embarrassing . . . and I'm hesitant about asking, but . . . still, I'm wondering what it all means.

BIG LEFTY
Dude; you're doing it again, Man. What do you mean *what it all means*?

PROFESSOR
Mr. Lefty, please excuse me for interjecting some clarity into this dialogue, but I think I'm beginning to comprehend our fellow, Spider's need and request.

Spider, are you asking for someone to explicitly tell the meaning of our story about puppet characters joined in a setting to experience events and overcome conflict? Are you asking for an omniscient voice to explicitly and concisely tell you a theme for the story we have been experiencing?

BIG LEFTY
Whoa, Dude, do you mean like with a fable? I know about fables, Man, because my friend the teacher tells fables to her students. And all her fables end the same way, Man, with . . . *the moral of this story is* . . . And then all her kids like know for sure the important like idea to get from the story. It's like way cool, Man.

PROFESSOR
Certainly, Mr. Lefty. A fable is an explicit approach at communication. It's a didactic form of literature intended to teach in a pleasant and entertaining manner, so it is quite reasonable that your teacher friend would choose to relate fables as part of her instructional presentation for young children. However, as we return to Spider's query, I am

fairly confident that we shall not come upon a fable-like moral within pages of *The Puppet Explained*. Probably to the contrary; for you see, Spider, each of us brings our own unique background and prior understandings to this story as it unfolds, and we must therefore discover its primary theme for ourselves. And Spider, there is also the possibility that this story, as is true of many others, may indeed have multiple themes. And therefore, Spider, the intellectual activity in which you have found yourself to be engaged is actually quite positive. Indeed, you are to be commended for using your mind in such fashion; certainly a Spider who contemplates theme is not one's stereotypical arachnid.

SPIDER
Oh, well then, I guess I won't worry that I've been wondering. I'll just go on about my business. But if I sometimes find myself wondering what it all means, I'll know it's okay to stop and think about theme for a while, and then when I'm done, I'll move on to something else.

PROFESSOR
That is splendid, Spider.

BIG LEFTY
Yeah, Spider, Dude. It's like totally cool, Man, if you wanta lean on one of your hairy legs or scratch your chin, Man. Wonder about stuff all you want, Man. No problemo.

MS. UP
YOO HOO! Here I am again. I bet you're going to be reeeeally surprised when I tell you that I think we just had another denouement. But I think it's totally true that we did.

Because when Spider said he realized that it's okay when he finds himself wondering, and decided he'll just let himself think about theme until he is done, I knew that his problem with wondering would be resolved. And golly; isn't that swell?

MADAME SILHOUETTE
Ahhh, my friends, I believe you, Ms. Up, are correct. Yes, another denouement has occurred. And now we who know dear Spider and value his character, stable, with kind and careful habits; we who also have need to find meaning; we, who from distant lands and diverse cultures have pondered as he; we now share dear Spider's relief in understanding activity of wonderment is natural within mind, and positive for well being.

Indeed, should Indonesian puppet play delight audience with sparkle through cuttings and perforations in silhouette shapes, yet not offer opportunity for understanding, the doing is wasted. Reassuring is that Spider will accept his inclination to wonder and also permit himself to move on to what lies ahead.

FINGER PUPPETS
Okay! We get it. And it's our turn. So let's celebrate another denouement!!!

Let's hear it for Spider! He knows it's okay to be wondering. When he's done, he'll do something else. It's natural. It's positive. Wowie! Zowie! Let's hear it for Spider! Yeah, Spider! Yeah!!! Whooop!

MR. RESILIENCY
Hello, there everyone. Seems like you puppets are having a good time. Mind if I join you? I've been looking forward to meeting you in person. I'm the guy Mr. Sock talked about earlier. Do you remember? I used to be just an ordinary, size 9-11 white athletic sock.

FINGER PUPPETS
Sure! We remember you! Hooray that you're here! Wowie! Zowie! You're just like Mr. Sock said!

SPIDER
Oh, hello. We're pleased to make your acquaintance, in person, I mean. I'd really like to shake your hand.

Oh, but you don't have one.

Oh, gosh. I hope I didn't make you feel uncomfortable because I noticed . . . that you don't have a hand, I mean.

Oh, my. Now I've gone and mentioned it so everyone else will notice, too.

Darn. Oh, I'm so sorry.

How about I just tip my derby? And please accept my apology. But I am very happy to meet you.

MR. RESILIENCY
Well, don't give it a second thought, Spider.

SPIDER
What brings you to this page?

MR. RESILIENCY
Actually, Spider, you're the reason I'm here. You see, Spider, I've been following what you said about wondering, and thought, "Well, this seems like a good time to introduce myself to fellow puppets, and join the conversation."

PROFESSOR
Then, welcome to you, Sir. I am the Professor. Indeed, we have been engaged in a most interesting dialogue around the concept of *theme*. Have you some comment to add that relates to our topic of conversation?

MR. RESILIENCY
Well, yes; as a matter of fact, I do. You may remember from what Mr. Sock had to say, and I'm sure it's hard to believe when you see me now, but there was a time when I'd really hit bottom. I know, it's difficult to even imagine when you see how I am today, but . . . at one point I was a hopeless sock, completely worn, worthless really.

Then everything changed for me when I was found by one of *them*. This one was creative. And through this one, a miracle happened for me; I was given a whole new chance at life—as a puppet.

So believe me; I'm a guy who's done his share of wondering. Yes, I have. I wondered about what it *means* when I was wrapped around a human foot. I wondered about what it *means* when I had to endure stretching, and what it *means* to endure scrunching, sweat, stink, laundry cycles, and drier heat. And I've wondered, "*So what?*" *So what* if I could endure through it all?

SPIDER
Oh, my. That is a lot of wondering. It makes my wondering seem insignificant.

MR. RESILIENCY

I can see that you're impressed, Spider, and believe me, I wasn't trying to brag about the amount of wondering I've done, or trying to make your wondering seem less important. I was just making a point, since the Professor here asked. And it is, that yes, I can definitely hold my own in a conversation about theme. Yes, for sure, I've given theme a lot of thought.

But now when I wonder, "What does it all mean?" or as Spider asked, "*So* what?" I've got a completely clear perspective. I actually find myself thinking that it means, "I *can* endure. Yes!"

And I find myself thinking the *so what* for enduring is that *I can tell my story*—of resiliency, and then others who face problems in life have a story they can hold on to—my story. You see, looking back, I realize that through one of *them*, I became a *character*. I've experienced many *settings*. I've played out *narrative order*. I've lived an assortment of *conflicts*. And I have survived *plots*, such that I am with you today, here on a page in *The Puppet Explained*. And now, when I think about what it all means in the really big picture, I know. I know it means . . . that socks . . . can be resilient.

"So what?" someone might ask. "So what?"

Well, to those folks, I will say loud and clear, "If a sock can make it, you can, too!"

BIG LEFTY

Whoa, like Survival Dude, like Resiliency Man, Sir, I'm in awe, Man, and you've got my respect, Dude. So, I've gotta ask, Man. Are you like saying that because you found a meaning in your own like story, Man, that there's a meaning in every story? Are you like suggesting that I, Big Lefty, should be able to figure out a *so what* for every story?

MR. RESILIENCY

Actually, Big Lefty, maybe not *every* story. Some stories might not give enough information to suggest a meaning. Some stories might leave you thinking, "So what?" for good reason.

CHAPTER 7

Who's Telling the Story?

MISS MUFFET
Hmm. Hmm. Excuse me, Mr. Resiliency, Sir. I have been sitting here on my comfortable tuffet, listening courteously, and not wanting to interrupt the conversation, however, you, Sir, just made a comment that causes me to wonder.

MR. RESILIENCY
Well, HELLO, Miss. Are you ever gorgeous! And your blue hair is incredible. Bet you get compliments all the time. Am I ever pleased to meet you, Miss!

MISS MUFFET
Oh. Hmm. Thank you. Hmm. I was about to say; hmm; you made a comment that has me wondering. You said, "Some stories might not give enough information to suggest a meaning." And I was wondering; hmm; I am wondering . . . how stories do that, I mean *give information*. I have not really thought about this before. But just how does a story give information?

BIG LEFTY
GEEZE, Man; like Miss Muffet, Man, it's another no brainer. With words, Man. A story gives information with like words.

MISS MUFFET
Oh, Mr. Lefty, I understand that a story gives information with words; of course. Everyone knows that, Mr. Lefty. But what I am wondering is . . . from where do the words come?

MS. UP
YOO HOO! It's me, Ms. Up, and this might be surprising, but I think I know. I'll be reeeeally happy to tell you, if you're ready.

MAROINETTE
I'm ready. I'm ready. I'm ready. And my strings'll tangle if I hafta wait for long.

FINGER PUPPETS
Okay! We're ready. Tell us, Ms. Up!!! Where? We can hardly wait! We're ready to celebrate! So tell us! Let's hear it for Ms. Up! Wowie! Zowie! Tell us, Ms. Up; tell us!

SPIDER
Oh, my, I'm certainly ready. It seems a lot of us are, Ms. Up, so please do tell us. How about on the count of eight?

SNAPPY
Deet Deet Deet Deet Deet Deet

Accurate N Concise, here, just as Ms. Up is about to answer a question posed by Miss Muffet.

Before Ms. Up responds, let's find out more about the question. Miss Muffet, in your own words, what was the question you asked?

MISS MUFFET
Oh, well, Mr. Concise, I asked, "From where do the words in a story come?"

SNAPPY
There you have it folks, the question posed by Miss Muffet. Now let's focus on Spider as he counts down for Ms. Up to respond.

SPIDER
Eight, seven, six, five, four, three, two, one!

MS. UP
Golly!!! Okay! Words come . . . Ready? . . . from . . . Reeeeally ready? . . . who ever is telling the story!!!

FINGER PUPPETS
Yeah! Yeah for Ms. Up!

Words . . . come . . . from . . . who . . . ever . . . is . . . telling . . . the . . . story . . . ! Yeah! Wowie! Zowie!

SNAPPY
Ladies and Gentlemen, there's a lot of energy in *The Puppet Explained* as Ms. Up has just responded to a question posed by Miss Muffet. Certainly the puppets here today were all eager to hear Ms. Up's response. Now let's turn to the Professor and get his reaction to what Ms. Up had to say.

Professor, we have just heard from Ms. Up that "Words come from who ever is telling the story." Could you elaborate for our audience?

PROFESSOR

Certainly, Mr. Concise. As you shall learn, elaboration is one of my acute professorial skills. To that end, your audience may find it interesting that unwittingly, Ms. Up, with Miss Muffet as an accomplice, has successfully provided segue to a literary term of genuine importance, that being *point of view*. You see, those words about which Miss Muffet inquired and for which Ms. Up provided a simplistic response, those words have been delivered by narration that was posed in one-of-four *points of view*. And a story's recipients will only obtain "information," as the former athletic sock put it, via one of those four. Indeed, everything that story recipients come to know about characters, setting, narrative order, conflicts, plot and themes will be filtered through a *point of view*.

SNAPPY

Well, that's interesting, Professor, but I'm afraid this commentator has run out of time. So, Ladies and Gentlemen, I'm Accurate N Concise, making an exit and it's back to you, Professor.

PROFESSOR

Yes; certainly, I shall continue. As I was explaining, one gleans information in a story through words that are delivered by narration which filters everything to be known through a particular point of view. There are four: first person, omniscient, limited omniscient, and the objective or dramatic point of view.

I shall provide examples to illustrate these four. Let's begin with the *first-person point of view*. It's as if everything is told in the first person "I." Say, for instance, Mr. Resiliency there relates a story thusly.

> I knew it would be a good day. I was feeling well, and it seemed to me the others were, too. I planned to do certain things and I did them. I saw others doing things and I can make guesses about what they had planned and what they might have accomplished. I have told you everything I want you to know. The End

MISS MUFFET
Hmm. Professor, but how shall we know what the other characters are thinking?

PROFESSOR
You shan't, Miss Muffet, unless the first person asks one of them directly, and then the first person tells you what the other person said in response.

MISS MUFFET
Oh. You are saying then, that when a story is told though a first-person point of view, the only information we are given will come through that person? I think I understand. Thank you, Professor.

PROFESSOR
You're welcome, Miss Muffet.

So now, on to another point of view, one called *omniscient*. Such a story is told in third person; that is as he, she, or they, by one who knows everything about everyone, past, present and future. The omniscient point of view can even inform a story's recipient about characters' unconscious thoughts.

BIG LEFTY
Whoa, that's far out, Man. Can you like give an example of that, Dude?

PROFESSOR
Certainly, Mr. Lefty.

> Even before he woke, somehow he knew it would be a good day. The sun wanted to wake him with its promising light, as it wanted to awaken all peoples and creatures. And when he woke, he felt well, even better than usual. They all did; people of every creed and creatures in every form. Why shouldn't they? There had never been any trouble and there never would be. And on this particular day, he had planned

to do certain things, just as his mother had hoped he would, even before he had been born. He saw others doing things. And while every one had been busy doing something uniquely different, still each was fulfilling a mother's hopes for her child. The End

BIG LEFTY
Cool, Man. Like how'd that point of view know everything, Man?

PROFESSOR
It is simple, Mr. Lefty; the point of view is omniscient.

BIG LEFTY
Like, whoa, Dude. That is far out and like way cool, Man.

PROFESSOR
So you appreciate an omniscient point of view, Mr. Lefty? Let's see how you respond to a third point of view, the limited omniscient. It too is told in third person, but the story only provides information and insights about characters of significance, such as follows.

He knew it would be a good day. He was feeling well. He planned to do certain things and did them. He saw others doing things, yet was focused on his own activities and what he might accomplish. He did his best. That's the kind of fellow he was. And at the end of his day, he was satisfied. The End

MISS MUFFET
Hmm. Professor, shall we get information about other characters?

PROFESSOR
Indeed, you may, Miss Muffet, but that information shall be limited, because they are of lesser importance. In a limited-omniscient point of view, focus is on one, or perhaps a very few major characters, and only their pasts, needs, behaviors, thoughts, and such are related in the story.

MISS MUFFET

Professor, it does seem the three points of view you have described provide different information. Will you please tell us about the fourth point of view that you mentioned?

PROFESSOR

Ah, yes, Miss Muffet, the objective or dramatic point of view. It can be explained thusly. Imagine that a camera is viewing a story. Every bit of information captured by the camera is available to a story recipient, who then draws conclusions about which images and sounds are worth noting. So interpretation is left to the story recipient. Permit me to share a story similar to the previous examples, yet told from an objective point of view.

> He opened his eyes, stretched his arms and threw off the covers. He said, "It will be a good day. I feel well, and can do just what I've planned." His lips were curved upwards in a smile. He went to the window and looked outside. Others were already outdoors. Someone said, "I can tell it's going to be a good day." Another one said, "Me, too. And I plan to get a lot done." He moved away from the window. A smile remained on his face. "I'm ready to get started," he said. The End

MARIONETTE

Okay, Okay, Okay; I think I get it. I get it. I get it.

Words . . . come . . . from . . . who . . . ever . . . is . . . telling . . . the . . . story . . . !, and whoever that is has a point of view, right? Right? Right? And point of view is like a lens. A lens. A lens. It's a filter. Right? Right? Am I right?

PROFESSOR

Good, fellow, Marionette. Yes, you're quite correct. Good fellow.

MARIONETTE

Swell; I thought I got it. I did. Yes, I did. I did.

Chapter 8

How Does It Feel?

BIG LEFTY

Hey, Dudes, could we like go back to like one of the stories? Because I've like had a thought that I wanta like put out there, Man.

SPIDER

Of, course, Big Lefty. I'd like to know what you're thinking. I'm sure all of us would. Say, let's have a show of hands and see how many of us would like to go back to a story, so Big Lefty can share his thought.

Oh. I forgot that some of us don't hand hands. Sorry, Mr. Resiliency; sorry, Mr. Sock.

BIG LEFTY

Geeeze, Spider. Like what about me, Man?

SPIDER

Oh, sorry, Big Lefty. Maybe that wasn't such a good idea.

FINGER PUPPETS

It's okay, Spider! We'll just speak for ALL the puppets. Yeah, Big Lefty! Let's go back! Tell us your thought! Tell us Big Lefty! Yeah!

BIG LEFTY

Far out, Dudes. So like here's my thought. Take the story from like that omniscient point of view. Like where the narrating dude like knew everything, from like way before, and like all over the place now, and like zoomed out into the future, Man. And say like words we get from that omniscient narrating dude are the only information we get about a story. Gettin' it so far? So like, what if this omniscient narrating dude is like completely like a negative dude? What if like everything the narrating dude says is like bleak and doom, Man; like from the totally dark side? You know? Like, I'll tell a story like the Professor did.

> Okay, so even before the dude woke, somehow like he knew it would be a horrible day. The sun like wouldn't shine, Man; so it like stayed dark. The rest of the dudes and creatures had to like get up in gloomy darkness, Man. And when this dude woke, he felt awful, even like more awful than usual. They all did, Man; people and creatures like in every form felt really awful. And like, of course they would. There had never, like NEVER been anything but trouble and there never would be—ever. The End

Get the picture? What if like the only information we get in the story is like from a point of view that's like a doom lens, Man?

MS. UP
Well, golly, Big Lefty, why would anyone want a story like that? It'd be reeeeally surprising if they did.

BIG LEFTY
Like yeah, I know, Ms. Up; I know, 'cause I'm like a cheerful dude, so I would like think it was weird, too, but I'm like trying to make a point, so like hang with me.

MS. UP
Oh, golly, I will hang with you, Big Lefty, and listen to your thought reeeeally carefully, I promise, but I'd like to just pop down for a while and listen from way inside my box, if you don't mind. I'd rather listen in my down position.

BIG LEFTY

Sure, Ms. Up; like whatever, but like I'm very close to making my point. Okay, so like say another story is like from the first-person point of view, and like all the words that like come through this first person, have like a chip-on-the-shoulder. You know what I mean?

> So it's like I knew this would be like another one of those days, Man. I was feeling fine, and like I'm as good as the next guy, but those other dudes seem to have all the breaks, Man. I like planned to do some stuff, and I like gave it my best shot, Man, but it's like what I do is never good enough, Man. Other dudes do the same stuff that I do, and they get like noticed, like they really accomplished something, Man. But ya know, I don't know why I even bother like to tell you, Man. It's like just unfair, Dude. The End

MISS MUFFET

Hmm, Hmm, Mr. Lefty. I am beginning to see your point; at least I think I am. I think you are saying that information we get about a story comes as words, through narration, which is presented from a certain point of view, and . . .

Ah. But, Mr. Lefty, let us please stop there for a moment, because that is already a lot about which to think. And I can not help fidgeting on my tuffet, which of course makes my pink, dotted-Swiss skirt get rumpled. And also, this amount of thinking can cause static around a brain, which is not nice on my usually-beautiful, blue hair.

So, I will take in a deep breath, and hold it. And then exhale, a full, cleansing breath.

And . . . now . . . now I am ready. Alright, Mr. Lefty, are you thinking that if there was more than one narration, even IF they were both told from the **same** point of view, they could be different? I mean, are you suggesting that an *attitude* could come through narration? Because a different attitude about the characters, or settings, or events could change the whole story. Could it not?

BIG LEFTY
Like yeah, Man; I mean Miss Muffet. Like I think that was my point.

MISS MUFFET
Well, then, I do see your point. So, what if we were to try an experiment? We could use the story you just told from the first-person point of view, and instead of having a chip-on-the-shoulder attitude, it could be told in a way that is cheerful.

BIG LEFTY
Far out idea, Man; I mean Miss Muffet. 'Cause like an experiment'd be cool, Man. And like, hey; for an experiment with cheerfulness, let's see if we can like get Ms. Up to help us.

MS. UP
YOO HOO! It's me! Ms. Up. I heard you say my name. You see, I was listening. And oh, golly, I'd reeeeally love to help you with an experiment. I've never done an experiment before. Do you think the Professor would let me borrow a lab coat and some beakers?

MISS MUFFET
Well, Ms. Up, it is not that kind of an experiment. All you will need to do is be your very cheerful self, and retell the first-person point of view story example in a cheerful way.

MS. UP
Oh, Golly Gee. I can do that without a lab coat and beakers. Easy! Here goes.

> Zippety do dah, I just knew it would be a reeeeally good day. I felt like popping up quickly, so I did, and oh, boy! Sure enough, everything I saw was in beautiful lighting and sparkly. And it seemed to me the others were ready for a good day, too. I had planned to do certain things and golly, what a perfect day for doing them. Actually, it was a perfect day for doing anything AND everything! So when I saw

others doing things, even though I could only guess about what they'd planned and accomplished, I'd be reeeeally surprised if it was anything less than wonderfully swell. So, golly; I've told you everything. The End

PROFESSOR
Very interesting, Miss Muffet, Ms. Up, and Mr. Lefty. You see, I have been listening to your conversation and I have observed your experiment. Truly, I think it was quiet remarkable that you chose to attempt an experiment, and I commend you for so doing. Permit me, if you will, to review; your hypothesis was?

BIG LEFTY
Oh, wow, Dude; I like need my teacher friend, Man, for hypothesis kinda stuff.

Okay. Wait. Okay. I . . . think, we thought, that a story could like be told from the like same point of view, Man, but like with a different attitude. Like that's it. Yes! And then if that's what happened, Man, then it'd like come across with a whole like different feeling. Yeah, Dude; that's the hypothesis.

PROFESSOR
Far out, Mr. Lefty. And what would you say was the result of your experiment?

MISS MUFFET
Hmmm, Mr. Lefty, may I respond to the Professor's question?

BIG LEFTY
Sure; like go for it.

MISS MUFFET
Well, Professor, I think our experiment showed that in this one instance, even though narration was though the same point of view, which was *first person*, a change in attitude definitely altered the feeling in our brief story.

PROFESSOR
Splendid, Miss Muffet, Ms. Up, and Mr. Lefty; splendid. For
you see, you have just demonstrated that what you referred to as
"attitude", and which is similar to what is called "tone" in discourse
about children's literature, plays an important part in every story.
"Tone" tells how the narrating voice or author of a story feels about
his or her subject, and about those receiving the story. A serious
tone communicates, "Let us be business like." A condescending
tone suggests that the story recipient is immature, ill informed, or
not intelligent. Whereas, a humorous tone says, "Let's have fun
together."

BIG LEFTY
So, Dude, are like *attitude* and *tone* like the same?

PROFESSOR
Well, Mr. Lefty, for our purposes, I will say, "Yes." Whosoever is
receiving a story, will be given information via words, presented
through a particular point of view, which is certainly tainted with
the tone or attitude of the story teller.

SPIDER
So, Professor, I've been wondering . . .

BIG LEFTY
Spider, Dude; again?

SPIDER
Well, I can't seem to help myself. I listen and get interested in what
puppets are saying, and before long, I think about something and
then I start wondering.

BIG LEFTY
Geeze, Dude.

PROFESSOR
Well, I for one am most pleased that Spider so frequently engages in
wondering. Indeed, Spider's wondering has prompted considerable

pondering and contemplation among puppet fellows, and such cognitive activity is too oft lacking, especially in this era of passive entertainment. And so I say, "Go for it, Spider!"

SPIDER
By that, Professor, do you mean it's alright for me to talk about what I'm wondering?

PROFESSOR
Most certainly, Spider, my good fellow. Please, tell us.

CHAPTER 9

Is This a Beginning?

SPIDER
Well, I was wondering . . . if I wanted to create a story, or one of the puppets here had a story to tell, or if we all decided to make up a story, where would we begin?

BIG LEFTY
Spider, Dude. It's like so way obvious, Man. We'd begin at the beginning, Man.

SPIDER
Well, Big Lefty, I think beginning at the beginning is a fine idea. I'm just wondering. When is the beginning? Is the beginning right now? Or is the beginning something that happened before now, that brought a story to right now?

BIG LEFTY
Whoa, Spider, like Dude, for an eight-legged ball, coated with flat, black paint, who is like t o t a l l y quiet a lot of the time, you sure do like to ponder and contemplate, Man.

SPIDER
Well, I was just thinking there could be things that happened before right now, that would be important to know. Some things that happened before could sort of explain why right now is like it is. And, another thing I thought about is that things which happened before, *if* we know about them, could kind of give clues as to what might happen in the beginning, and even after the beginning.

PROFESSOR

Spider, perhaps you mean that information told prior to the beginning of a story line could *foreshadow*, or give clues to what is about to transpire within a narration.

SPIDER

Oh. Well. I guess that's what I mean. And also, I mean that a story could begin with right now, and get everything going, and then jump back to what happened before the beginning.

PROFESSOR

Yes, that could happen, Spider. It often does. It's called a *flashback*, and it is one way of giving more complete information to those receiving the story.

SPIDER

So, that is in a way what I mean. A story could begin at a beginning right now, but really begin with something that happened before now.

PROFESSOR

Spider, dear fellow, I think one could accurately say that a story could begin at any point, and does begin then.

BIG LEFTY

Far out, Man. It begins when it begins. Now I like understand it in a whole new way, Man. And it makes everything so much bigger; a story doesn't have to begin like at the plain old beginning that's right now, Man; it could begin whenever. That is way cool. Far out, Man. And geeze, thanks, Spider, for goin' there, Man. Far out!

MS. UP

Oh, YOO HOO! Hello! I'm up again. You probably forgot about me while I went back into my down position, because I was quiet before I popped up again; BUT, now I'm right here. And I popped up because I have something I reeeeally want to talk about that's important.

SPIDER

Oh, Ms. Up. I'm pretty sure that we didn't forget about you, and it's swell for you to take time from your down position to pop up and say things.

MS. UP

Golly, Spider. I love popping up because it's reeeeally bright out here in my up position with light everywhere. I love popping up and I also love light. Wowie! Zowie! And I especially love popping up when I have something to talk about with my new friends.

PROFESSOR

Ms. Up, you appear to be even more, I think the word is *enthusiastic* than usual. What is it that you are so eager to talk about with your fellow puppets?

MS. UP

Well, golly, Professor. Do you remember when Spider helped me realize that something was missing for me and what was missing wasn't as simple as setting? Spider helped me realize that all my up-ing and down-ing gave no story line. And then you, Professor, helped me realize that I also needed to have some conflict so there could be plot in my life, and then I finally said, "Golly, Gee!!! I will. I will be open to possibilities and look for interesting plots wherever I might be." And then everyone got excited because I showed some spirit and the finger puppets were cheering, "YEAH, Ms. Up!!!" And "BRAVO!"

PROFESSOR

Indeed, Ms. Up. I do recall that sequence of events, as will most of our puppet fellows. And so, Ms. Up, what do you supposed has given you such verve at this moment . . . and caused you to take your up position so suddenly after retiring to your more private down situation?

MS. UP

Well, Professor. Some of you were talking about *when a story begins*. That made me think about narrative order, which made me think about conflict. Next I thought about denouements. And then . . .

well, golly, Professor, I had a giant thought. Want to know what it was?

PROFESSOR
Oh yes, Ms. Up. And I think I can speak for our fellow puppets. We most certainly do want to know your *giant thought*.

MS. UP
Okay. Well; I think it's a reeeeally important thought. So if you're ready . . .

FINGER PUPPETS
Oh, we are, Ms. Up. Yeah for your thought! We are really ready. Yeah!!! Tell us, Ms. Up; tell us!!!

MS. UP
Let's not even count down from eight; I'll just tell you my thought, which is more of a question, but I'll just say it anyway.

PROFESSOR
Yes, Ms. Up. Please proceed. Do not stop the momentum.

Chapter 10

Is It Finished?

MS. UP

Okay. So, golly, here's my thought or I guess it's a question. "When does a story end?"

BIG LEFTY

Oh, geeze, Dude, I mean, Ms. Up; you're actin' like Spider, nothing personal, Man.

SPIDER

It's quite okay, Big Lefty. No offense taken.

BIG LEFTY

Thanks, Man. So, like Ms. Up, Dude; think about it, Man; a story ends when it's over.

MS. UP

Oh, golly; I understand that, Big Lefty. After all I learned about narrative order and conflict and plot and denouement. I'm thinking that a story is over when it's over. Only, golly; does everything really end when a story is over? What I mean is, what will happen to characters when it's over? Because, golly; just think about it. When a story ends . . .

So, golly gee, I'm hoping that characters will live happily ever after. But when I started to think about this, I realized that it might not work out that way when a story ends. For example, I personally, rather than living happily ever after with conflicts and everything, I might just stay in my down position for ever more.

MISS MUFFET

Well, Ms. Up, is not it possible that some characters might just continue as they were for long after a story ends, because they will be remembered. They might be remembered for sparkle in their eyes, or remembered for their hair, or remembered for what they have said, or things others said about them; some characters might just have truly enduring personalities and be remembered for ever more.

SPIDER

Ms. Up, now you've got me thinking that when a story ends, I hope things won't go back to the way they were before a story started. Take me for example. I wouldn't want things to go back to like they were before I found my blue, wool derby, when if I was noticed, others would shriek and some would try to hit me with a shoe. When the story ends, I wouldn't want to have to go back to hiding in boring places like wood piles and start being shy again.

BIG LEFTY

Now wait a minute, Spider. Why would things hafta change, Man? Just because a story is like over? Nothing's gonna change about me, Dude. I'm gonna be Big Lefty no matter what, Man. I might look like a hand at the end of somebody's arm, Man, but I'm still gonna have my mouth and I'm still gonna use it. I might like lay low, hide out, until another story comes along, Man, but one will, and then like Big Lefty returns, Man. Right on!

SNAPPY

Deet Deet Deet Deet Deet Deet

Accurate N. Concise, here, live from pages of *The Puppet Explained*, where a provocative question—When does a story end?—has puppets engaged in conversation. These puppets seem to have focused on concern about *what happens to characters* when a story ends. For complete and uncensored coverage of this dialogue, I am at the scene, speaking directly with those involved. Let me see if I can get Ms. Up, the puppet who sparked this conversation, to make a comment.

Ms. Up! Ms. Up!

MS. UP
Oh; golly! It's Snappy. Hello, Snappy!

SNAPPY
And, hello to you, Ms. Up. Would you be willing to say a few words about the conversation you're having with fellow puppets?

MS. UP
Oh, sure, Snappy. Well, Golly, Gee!!! I guess I should *begin* by saying that a while ago I was involved in a denouement, and ever since then I've been open to possibilities; you know, about things that could be interesting plots.

SNAPPY
Yes, Ms. Up, as the commentator covering that story, I know it was accurately reported and discussed concisely.

MS. UP
Oh, golly then, Snappy. Want me to tell you the next parts?

SNAPPY
Please do, Ms. Up. I'm here for complete and uncensored coverage.

MS. UP
Oh, okay. Well, you see, I was in my down position and heard puppets talking about when a story begins, which got me thinking about when a story ends. Now, before my denouement, I would probably have just stayed in my down position and not popped up to get involved with something that might possibly become an interesting plot.

SNAPPY
Yes, Ms. Up; that was before, and what has happened now?

MS. UP
Well, I asked about what will happen to characters when a story is over? Because, golly; just think about it. When a story ends . . . and that question actually made others begin thinking about what will happen to characters when a story is over. It seems that some have taken the question reeeeally personally.

SNAPPY
There you have it, directly from Ms. Up, who posed a question that now has puppets thinking and talking. Thank you, Ms. Up.

MS. UP
Oh, golly; you're welcome, Snappy; any time.

SNAPPY
Alright, and now let's go to Mr. Sock, and hear what he has to say about when a story ends, and possible consequences for characters when it does.

Mr. Sock. Oh, Mr. Sock! I'm Accurate N. Concise, here to report on the conversation puppets are having about when a story ends, and more specifically, what might happen to characters. Mr. Sock, would you mind telling us your thoughts?

MR. SOCK
Sure, I'm happy to tell you, Snappy. Isn't that what you like to be called?

SNAPPY
Yes, Mr. Sock, please call me Snappy.

MR. SOCK
Sure, Snappy; will do. So, the way I see it is like this. There have always been stories. And they all end. But it's a sure thing that almost the very same stories will be retold or read again some time

down the road. It's a lot like socks. They're inside shoes, folded and closed in drawers, stuck in a hampers with who knows what others, agitated in washers, and subjected to drier cycles, but the fact is, most socks make it. You want to know my stance, Snappy? Here it is. Stories will end, but I'm not worried about what will happen to characters. I think most characters are like socks.

SNAPPY

Well, that's certainly something to think about, Mr. Sock. Thank you. And now, I see the Marionette. Let's hear what he has to say.

MARIONETTE

Oh, good. It's my turn. Good. Good. Good. Because I'm kinda, sorta, a bit worried that when a story ends, marionettes will be mostly, kinda, just sorta left hanging, and I'm a little concerned, at least somewhat, well actually quite a bit, that when a story ends we'll be left with nothing to do and our strings will get knotted and we'll just be collecting dust.

SNAPPY

There you have it, directly from the Marionette, and thank you, Sir.

The marionette made a statement about possibilities that could be tragic, and if a character here in *The Puppet Explained* is concerned, doubtless there are characters elsewhere who also worry, although their numbers and the extent of their worries has not yet been determined.

But in order to provide thorough coverage of this evolving situation, this commentator will interview everyone who is available, and here near us now is Madame Silhouette.

Excuse me, Madame Silhouette, I am Accurate N. Concise, reporting through pages of *The Puppet Explained*.

MADAME SILHOUETTE

Hello, Mr. Concise. It is pleasure to meet you.

SNAPPY
Thank you, Madame Silhouette. So, you are a shadow puppet from Indonesia, is that correct?

MADAME SILHOUETTE
Yes, Mr. Concise, and I am most pleased to be here, enjoying time and listening to conversation of fellow puppets.

SNAPPY
That's good, Madame Silhouette, and precisely why my audience will benefit from getting your perspective. So, please tell us you thoughts regarding when a story ends?

MADAME SILHOUETTE
Oh, in my way of thinking, a story—that is good story—will not end. Story will finish, because it is satisfying to have finish. But good story will be told and heard again many times.

SNAPPY
That is interesting, Madame Silhouette. And what do you think might happen to characters at the finish of a story?

MADAME SILHOUETTE
Oh, Mr. Concise. It is interesting what might happen to characters. Well, I believe characters may live—for much time after story is finished—and live even before story is retold. Oh, characters could be fine ones, like strong and brave, or very nasty, but I believe once characters have been known, they may live on, even without print to tell about them.

SNAPPY
Thank you, Madame Silhouette, for your enlightening perspective.

MADAME SILHOUETTE
You are welcome, Mr. Concise. The pleasure was mine.

SNAPPY
And now let's check in with the finger puppets.

FINGER PUPPETS

Hey, Mr. Concise. We're ready for you. We've been listening to this conversation about when a story ends and what happens to characters when it does. Right, Guys?

Yes!!! We've been listening! And thinking! And talking among ourselves!

So, Mr. Concise, as you can see, there are a lot of us. And we really haven't reached consensus about when we think a story ends, or about what we think happens to characters when it does. But, we drew straws to decide that I should be our spokesperson when talking with you.

Yeah, we have a spokesperson! You can do it! Speak for all of us!!!

SNAPPY

Well, being a commentator, I'll attest that you have backing from all these finger puppets. As spokesperson then, 1) What do finger puppets think about when a story ends? And 2) What do you think happens to characters when a story ends?

FINGER PUPPETS

Super questions. And as finger puppets we are so happy to have a chance to respond. That is so great! And we all thank you. And as finger puppet spokesperson, for your questions 1 and 2, I get to tell you that we don't know. But we are glad to have been asked.

SNAPPY

Well, there it is, the collective thinking of finger puppets regarding when a story ends and what happens to characters when it does.

I'm Accurate N. Concise on location in *The Puppet Explained*, continuing with puppet interviews, and moving along to Mr. The Spoon. Sir, will you please tell us when you think a story ends?

MR. THE SPOON

Yes. I will. It ends when it is over.

SNAPPY
Well, thank you, The. That is your first name, isn't it? The?

MR. THE SPOON
Yes. The is my given name.

SNAPPY
Well, The, what do you think happens to characters when a story ends?

MR. THE SPOON
They wait.

SNAPPY
Alright, then. Thank you, The. That's a succinct and no doubt informed response.

There are two more on-the-scene-puppets to interview for complete and uncensored coverage of this dialogue. And next we have Mr. Resiliency.

MR. RESILIENCY
Hey, there, Snappy. I suppose you're cool with being addressed casually by a fellow celebrity. I'll bet you plan to do another interview, finding out what puppets think about when a story ends and then what happens to characters when a gig is complete.

SNAPPY
Yes, Mr. Resiliency, that is my intent. So, what can you tell us?

MR. RESILIENCY
Sure. Well, you may remember from what Mr. Sock shared, that I'm one who really hit bottom; and nobody wants to be there. But a story ending is not the same as hitting bottom. A story ending is something very different; it's completion—completion, which is a good thing.

And let me tell you, I have completed my share of stories, and many of them were dramatic; I have lived tragic roles. But, ask me what happens to a character when a story ends. Well, I'm absolutely confident that any character worth knowing will just be 100% ready for another story.

SNAPPY
Thank you, Mr. Resiliency.

MR. RESILIENCY
Sure thing, Snappy.

SNAPPY
And last in this interview series is the distinguished Professor. Sir, a moment of your time please, to learn your thoughts on when a story ends

PROFESSOR
Certainly, Mr. Concise. However, let me first provide information that has either been insufficiently stated, or perhaps has not been retained. You see, many stories, although not all, involve some sort of conflict between a main character or protagonist, and some antagonist. I hope my fellow puppets will recall that we spoke earlier about sources of conflict, when we were trying to clarify Ms. Up's situation and discomfort.

At that time it was explained that another person, nature, society or one's self could be possible sources of conflict. I mention this, because it is when that conflict has been brought to a climax, Mr. Concise, when the conflict has been addressed and met squarely for a clear sense of resolution, that a story has a comfortable closed ending.

However, in other fictional stories, although not many, a climax and resolution are not as obvious and tidy. Indeed, a story's ending may actually be left open, for recipients to draw their own conclusions. In either approach, the story ends.

SNAPPY

Thank you, Professor, for that information, which I'm certain was widely appreciated. Just a bit more of your time, Professor, to please tell us what you think happens after a story ends, especially in regard to the characters.

PROFESSOR

Well, Mr. Concise, we puppets have previously dialogued regarding the word theme, which comes from the Greek and literally means something *laid down*; something of significance; something memorable that can be taken away from the story. So, Mr. Concise, I submit, that with a story's end, a theme may linger.

SNAPPY

That seems logical, Professor. So, now please tell us about the characters. What might we expect will happen with them?

PROFESSOR

Mr. Concise, I hesitate in responding to that question, for you see, I suspect that what happens to characters depends almost entirely upon the individuals, but I have no substantial or objective basis to presume so. I have not conducted research related to the question of what happens with characters subsequent to a story ending, nor do I know that colleagues have approached such study

SNAPPY

I see, Professor. And as a commentator, I do understand your hesitancy; it would be irresponsible for me to report something that's less than factual. So, thank you for telling us what you could, Professor. And that completes the interviews and uncensored coverage of dialogue in most recent pages of *The Puppet Explained*. This has been . . .

BIG LEFTY

Hey, wait a minute, Snappy, Dude. Not so fast, because I've got an idea.

SNAPPY
Oh. Yes. Speaking now is Big Lefty, for those of you who may not recognize this puppet from a previous interview. So, Big Lefty, you say you have an idea.

BIG LEFTY
Yeah, Man, and it's like so obvious, Man, because you just heard the Professor say there's not like research done on what happens to characters when a story ends, Man.

SNAPPY
Yes, Big Lefty. That is what the professor told us.

BIG LEFTY
So, my idea is to do an experiment, Man. We'll like, end this story and then find out what happens to all the characters.

PROFESSOR
Mr. Lefty, at times you astound me. That's a splendid idea. It's a most original research topic, which should generate a great deal of scholarly interest and result in perhaps multiple publication opportunities. Of course, we'll need to conduct the experiment using appropriate methodology such that it can be replicated. But that is not a problem; I'll see to it.

So, what say you, fellow puppets? Shall we resolve our question about what happens to characters when a story ends by engaging in an experiment?

MISS MUFFET
Oh, yes. I think we should. It is just such an exciting idea, being in an experiment with Spider and Mr. Lefty, and all the rest of you. Oh, just look at me. My hands are trembling and my eyes must be sparkling wildly. Oh, I feel like swooning into the fullness of my pink, dotted-Swiss skirt!

BIG LEFTY
Well, don't swoon yet, Dudette, 'cause like we need to have methodology, Man, like the Professor said.

MISS MUFFET
Oh, yes. Please excuse me. It is just such an exciting idea. I will do my deep breathing and calm myself. No need to worry.

SPIDER
That's good, Miss Muffet, because I think an experiment is a great idea. I'd like to find out for sure that things won't be like they were before the story started. But, if an experiment proved that it would, then I would know and could take some action before my derby was gone and I reverted back to the old Spider's way of life.

MR. RESILIENCY
That's the spirit, Spider! Be proactive!

SPIDER
Well, thank you, Mr. Resiliency.

MS. UP
Oh, YOO HOO! It's me again. I popped up, because I'm willing to do the experiment. You know that I am open to possibilities!

PROFESSOR
Splendid, Ms. Up. And what say you, Marionette?

MARIONETTE
For sure, Professor. I'm for it! Count me in. I'm ready. Just so long as we get started, and I don't get tangled.

PROFESSOR
And you, Madame Silhouette; will you agree to conducting an experiment?

MADAME SILHOUETTE
Professor, I will be most pleased to participate with fellow puppets.

PROFESSOR
Splendid, Madame; thank you.

PROFESSOR
Ah, and Mr. Spoon, The, what is your position?

MR. THE SPOON
Right now, I am vertical.

MS. UP
Oh, The, golly gee. I didn't know you could be funny. I thought you were a straight man. Tee Hee!

MR. THE SPOON
He asked. I answered.

PROFESSOR
Ah, let me pose a different question for Mr. Spoon. The, my good fellow, would you consider joining other puppets in an experiment?

MR. THE SPOON
Yes.

PROFESSOR
Yes, you will consider? Or yes, you will join the experiment?

MR. THE SPOON
Both. I *am* a puppet.

PROFESSOR
Oh, certainly, The, and rightfully aligned with your fellows. Splendid.

FINGER PUPPETS
Hey! Don't forget us! We'll be in the experiment! The more the merrier! Whoopee!!!

PROFESSOR
Oh, grand. And that leaves Mr. Sock and Mr. Resiliency. What say you fellows about participation?

MR. SOCK and MR. RESILIENCY
We're in for sure.

PROFESSOR
Well, I think we have heard from everyone and all are in agreement about implementing Mr. Lefty's idea regarding an experiment to determine what happens with characters after the conclusion of a story.

FINGER PUPPETS
Yeah!!!!! Let's do it!!!!

MISS MUFFET
Oh. Oh my. This is just too exciting!

PROFESSOR
Steady, Miss Muffet, compose yourself so that you are able to participate.

MISS MUFFET
Oh, yes. Thank you, Professor. I will just sit down right here and do deep breathing. I do not want to miss any of this.

PROFESSOR
Very good, Miss Muffet. Now, my fellows, the catalyst for what transpires during this experiment will be ending the story. It is essential that you simply conduct yourselves naturally, such that subsequent behaviors are true to character. I will make observations with as much objectivity as possible, and record that data. And at this time, it is appropriate for *Snappy* here to report on our activity.

SNAPPY
Thank you, Professor.

Deet Deet Deet Deet Deet Deet

Breaking news, here, live and direct from pages of *The Puppet Explained*, where the story is ending. All of us will just have to wait and see what happens when it has ended, and of course there is real interest in what will happen with characters. This has been Accurate N. Concise, AKA Snappy. And it's back to you.